I0630218

Inca Wraith

The Young Explorers, Volume 1

S T Cameron

Published by Bakaloo Media, 2025.

To request permission, contact Bakaloo Media - info@bakaloo.com.

Cover By Milan Jovanovic

Edited By Susan Hozak

Inca Wraith / S T Cameron. – 2nd ed.

ISBN 13: 979-8-88623-014-7

*To Chloe, Julian, Mae and Jarrett
for whom I wrote these stories*

Chapter 1

Inca Empire, Spring 1532.

Mani opened his eyes and blinked. Sunlight already streamed around the cloth hanging across the hut's doorway. The eleven-year-old stretched and breathed in the smell of corn and chili peppers lingering from dinner the night before.

Then he sat bolt upright. He was late.

Getting up from the mat where he slept, he slipped on his tunic and sandals. He wolfed down the cornbread still sitting on the table and eyed the pair of pichqa next to it.

The pichqa were dice made of wood carved into the shape of an elongated pyramid with six sides. A unique symbol on each side indicated the score. It was one of Mani's favorite games.

But the time to play had passed, so he ran out into the mid-morning sun to find his father, who would be furious.

He glanced at the terraces that were carved into the mountainside. They created steps that ran to the town far below, nestled between the foot of the mountain and the ocean. Many people worked on the terraces, planting maize, potatoes, and other vegetables that supplied the town with food. His mother and little brother had been working out there since sunrise while he slept.

He started up the path to the temple and stopped. Looking down the mountainside at the town, he saw smoke billowing above the buildings and strange ships anchored in the harbor.

The smoke and the ships frightened the boy. He hurried to find his father. He would know what was happening.

The Inca Emperor put Anka, Mani's father, in charge of building the largest temple in their province. They built the temple on a bluff high above the city and dedicated it to Inti, the god of the sun. They weren't done, but his father told him they would finish by Mani's twelfth year, only three new moons away.

Behind the temple, carved into the mountain, was the foot of a giant pyramid. They used the inside as a sacred burial place, but it would be years before they finished the outside.

Mani hurried up the steps to the temple door. He found his father inside, talking with two men who helped supervise the temple construction.

Anka glanced over at his son when he entered and frowned at him. Mani lowered his gaze and waited for his father by the temple entrance. His father would scold him before giving him his duties for the day.

Mani was glad he was an apprentice to his father rather than working in the fields all day, like his mother and brother. Still, working in the fields might be better than facing his father's anger.

The two men finished talking with Anka and hurried out of the temple. He strode over and looked down at his son. His eyes were dark as he glared at the boy.

"I'm sorry, Father," Mani said. "I have no excuse." He bowed his head.

"Don't let it happen again," his father said. Mani braced himself for a scolding, but his father said no more about it. "Come," he said, "we must prepare for the festival tomorrow." He led the boy through the large room toward the altar.

"There's smoke in the city," the boy said.

"In the city?"

"Yes, and strange ships."

His father stopped and looked at him curiously. He glanced over his shoulder at the temple entrance.

"Come with me," he said, leading Mani out of the temple and onto the plaza at the top of the steps. They looked down at the city filled with smoke and the ships just offshore from the town.

A man ran toward them from the city. He hurried across the rope bridge that spanned the gully between the terraces and the plateau where the temple was being built.

Mani didn't recognize the man, but his father did.

"Chaski," he greeted the man. "What news do you have?"

The man rushed up to them, out of breath and sweating profusely. It was several moments before he could speak.

"The city, Anka," he said between breaths. "It is under attack."

"Who is attacking the city?" Anka asked.

"I don't know. They came in enormous ships," the man said, pointing at the harbor. The ships were flying white flags with two crossed red bars.

"What do they want?"

"They are looking for gold and silver."

Mani saw many warriors marching up the road from the city toward the temple. They wore armor and had swords hanging on their belts or in their hands. The smoke over the city behind them was growing thicker and darker.

The boy looked at his father.

Anka stood silent in thought.

"They will desecrate the tombs," Chaski said. "They will steal from the dead."

Some warriors went into the fields. The men dragged women and older boys to their feet and spoke to them. They pushed them back down to the ground. Each time, a blade would flash, and they would not get up. They ignored small children and left them to fend for themselves.

"Father!" Mani pulled on the man's tunic urgently. "They are killing them," he cried, pointing toward the fields.

His father nodded. He kneeled in front of the boy. "I need you to come with me. You have an important task to do."

Mani looked at his father. If he could do something meaningful to help his people, he would.

Anka led him out the rear door of the temple and hurried up the path toward the pyramid entrance.

Mani saw his father glance back down the mountain several times, and each time he did, he hurried faster. The boy ran to keep up with his father.

When they reached the entrance to the pyramid, Anka kneeled in front of his son and clasped him by the shoulders.

"Why is this important?" he asked, gesturing to the pyramid under construction.

"It is a sacred burial ground. We place our elders inside for their journey into the afterlife."

"That is correct," his father said. "And it falls to you to help protect this sacred place."

Mani forced a smile despite the fear that caused him to shake. He was glad that his father was giving him such an important job.

Mani's father stood and took him to an alcove beside the door. He showed the boy a wooden lever.

"If those warriors come near here, pull this lever."

Mani looked confused. His father continued. "It will close the door to the pyramid and seal them out. Once it is closed, they won't be able to desecrate this place. Do you understand?"

Mani nodded.

His father put his hand on the boy's shoulder. "I'm proud of you, son," he told him.

Anka turned and rushed back toward the temple.

Mani wanted to go with his father. He wished he could stand with his father when he confronted the warriors. And he wanted to help protect the temple. But he knew that guarding the pyramid was important. And his father left that task to him.

Mani saw four men who worked with his father come running out to meet him. They carried spears and gestured behind them wildly. One man handed his father a spear, and together they stood facing the temple door.

A group of warriors appeared at the door. They slowly approached the five men. Mani heard them speak, but could not make out what they were saying. More warriors appeared from either side of the building and surrounded the five men.

Mani's heart was beating wildly. His father and the other men had spears, but the other warriors had swords. He wanted to yell to his father, to tell him to run away.

The leader of the warriors stepped forward to talk to Anka. The four other men stood between the warrior leader and his father.

Mani could see anger on the leader's face. He shouted at Anka, but his father shook his head.

The leader gestured at the men standing before him, blocking his way with their spears. Several of the warriors stepped forward with long sticks that looked like horns. They pointed the horns at the four men, and Mani saw smoke pour out of them.

There was the sound of thunder. All four men fell backward onto the ground and didn't move. Mani's father stood alone against the warriors.

Anka held his spear at the leader, who strode over the bodies of the four dead men. His father stabbed the spear at the leader, but it didn't go into him. He tried again. It just glanced off his armor and slid uselessly to the side.

The leader drew his sword from the sheath and brought it down on the spear. The spear splintered and broke in half. Then the sword came swinging back.

Anka dropped the broken spear and fell to his knees, clutching his stomach. He looked at the warrior and then fell forward into the dirt.

Mani screamed when he saw his father fall. He took several steps forward to go to him, but then stopped himself. Stumbling, he fell to his knees. His eyes filled with tears, and sickness flooded through him. He vomited into the dirt.

He screamed again and looked toward his father through blurry eyes.

The leader pointed up at the pyramid. The warriors ran up the hill toward him.

They were almost upon him when he remembered the task that his father had given him. It was the last thing his father asked him to do.

He scrambled to his feet and rushed to the lever.

He pulled it with all his might. It slowly moved and then came loose. He pushed it all the way down. With a low rumbling, the stone door lowered slowly down to block the entrance to the pyramid.

Mani looked down the path. The warriors were almost there. His father was still lying motionless on the ground near the temple, and although he couldn't see them, he knew his mother and brother were lying in the dirt of the terraces. Their spirits were on a journey into the afterlife, along with his father's spirit.

He saw the swords of the warriors flashing in the morning sun and knew he would soon join them. He glanced at the door. It was almost closed. The door would protect the dead from desecration. Soon, his task would be complete.

But what if they opened the pyramid? He couldn't protect the pyramid if he were dead.

He had an idea. His task was to protect the dead, so that's what he would do.

He ran toward the door, ducking under the swords of the first warriors. He dropped to the ground and rolled under the door into the pyramid. A blade slashed under the door and cut him deeply, but it snapped when the door fell into place. The boy sat bleeding in the silent darkness of the tomb.

Chapter 2

Wakina, Minnesota, June 8, 1917

A little after three in the morning, a Packard pulled up in front of a white house with a picket fence. The car had picked up dust traveling the dirt roads from the badlands of North Dakota back home to Wakina, Minnesota, and the seven days' worth of dust caused the dark red finish to look dull gray. The car chugged several times and then let out a hiss as the engine shut off.

Angus Kask removed his round spectacles and cleaned the dust off them. He looked across at his son, C.J., sleeping on the passenger side of the seat. The eleven-year-old was an immense help to his father. He had already learned much about archaeology on the seven expeditions he'd been on. Not seven, his father corrected himself. It was eight. He smiled at the boy and got out of the car.

Angus let the boy sleep as he unpacked their things and brought them into the house. When the car was empty, he shook the boy to wake him up.

"Where are we?" C.J. asked as he uncurled his body and stretched his legs. "It's still dark."

"We're home," Angus told him. "Go in and get some proper sleep."

The boy walked ahead of his dad into the house. He kicked off his shoes and mumbled, "Hi, Mom. We're back," to the portrait above the fireplace before going into the kitchen for a drink of water.

The portrait, a photograph of C.J. when he was seven with both his parents, was the only photograph they had of C.J.'s mother before she passed away a year later. His father always said that C.J. took after her with his sandy blond hair and blue eyes.

"Are you hungry?" Angus asked his son.

"A little," C.J. said, dropping into a kitchen chair.

"Eggs?"

"Eggs."

They were finishing the early breakfast when there was a pounding on the front door.

"Odd time for visitors," his father said, looking at the clock. It was four-thirty. He glanced at his son. "Go up and get some sleep. Leave the dishes. I'll take care of them later."

C.J. nodded and went to the stairs. He paused for a moment to see who was visiting so early.

Angus glanced out the window and opened the front door with a heavy sigh. Two men in brown suits and carrying briefcases stood on the doorstep.

"Good morning, Dr. Kask," one of them said. The two men nodded in greeting.

"Wesgrave," Angus greeted the first one. He turned to the second. "And Young. How nice to see you both."

Both men knew it wasn't.

"May we come in?" Wesgrave asked. He removed his hat, exposing short-cropped snow-white hair.

"I guess there's no avoiding it," Angus said, stepping back to allow them in.

The two men entered.

"Where can we talk?" Young asked. The man's name could not have been any more wrong. He had to be at least eighty, if not older.

"Why don't we go to my study?" Angus said, waving a hand toward the French doors that opened from the living room.

He saw C.J. had not gone upstairs yet. "Go on up and get some sleep," he told him again, waving him off.

C.J. wasn't sleepy anymore. Curious about the men, he wanted to see why they were visiting his father at that hour. Waiting until the doors to his father's study closed, he carefully crossed the room, trying to avoid any known creaky floorboards.

When he reached the doors, he kneeled by a heating grate. The grate allowed the heat from the coal furnace to come up from the

basement and warm both the living room and the study. It also allowed
C.J. to hear what they said in the other room.

"How are things at the Chicago Museum of Archaeology?" C.J.
heard his father ask.

"As it always is," Mr. Young said.

"Angus, we're here on museum business," Wesgrave said.

"I didn't think you were making a social visit," Angus said. "A visit
from the pair of you always means trouble for me."

"Trouble is your specialty," Young told him.

Angus sighed. "What can I do for you on this bright and cheerful
morning?" he asked.

A briefcase snapped open, and some papers rustled as the men
passed them around. The room was quiet while Angus glanced at them.
After several minutes, C.J. heard them drop back down on the desk.

"OK," Angus said. "Just give me the facts."

"Last year, we authorized an archaeological expedition to the
Republic of Peru in South America," Wesgrave said.

"You authorized it?" Angus asked.

"By we, I mean the museum, of course," Wesgrave said. He sounded
annoyed at Angus's literalness.

"Go on," Angus told him.

"There is a site south of Lima where they found ruins of an Inca
temple. We sent some men down there to do some preliminary work
on the site," Young said.

"Who did you send?" Angus asked.

"Potter and Freitag," Wesgrave said.

"Freitag?" Angus asked.

"Yes, Freitag," Wesgrave said. "I know you have a history with him,
but—"

"That's all in the past," Angus said.

"Does Freitag think so?" Young asked.

C.J.'s father didn't reply.

"Anyway," Young continued, "they left three months ago. We received the standard weekly reports."

"What did they find?" Angus asked.

"Nothing unusual. They said it appeared to be a temple of Inti, the Inca god of the sun," Young told him. "Several weeks into the survey, we received a cable saying they had discovered what appeared to be a pyramid cut into the mountain behind the temple."

"Interesting," Angus said.

"Very," Young said. "Three weeks ago, we received word that they had found what might be the door into the pyramid. They planned to open it."

"Did they?" Angus asked.

"We don't know," Wesgrave said. "That was the last we heard from them."

There was a pause.

"So, you want me to go down there and find out what kind of trouble they've gotten themselves into," Angus said.

"That's the idea," Wesgrave said.

"I just got back from a site in North Dakota. I'm exhausted," Angus told them.

"You'll get double your normal fees," Young said.

"You must be very interested in this pyramid," Angus said. C.J. didn't hear the two men respond.

It remained quiet for several minutes.

"Where are you staying?" Angus asked them.

"There is a hotel across town," Wesgrave told him. "I think it's called the Parker."

"Let me call Roland," Angus said. "I'll see if I can arrange it."

"We hope you can," Young said.

"Either way," Angus said, "I'll call the front desk of the Parker in an hour."

C.J. heard the men getting to their feet. He jumped up and dashed across the room. He ducked into the kitchen just as the study doors opened.

"We will wait for your call," Wesgrave said.

Angus opened the front door for them. "I'll be in touch," he told them.

After they left, he returned to his study, and C.J. heard him crank up the telephone.

C.J. couldn't believe it when they installed the telephone. They were one of the first houses in Wakina to get one. It made all of his friends jealous. His excitement was short-lived, though, when he found that there wasn't anyone to call. No one else he knew had one.

"Roland?" C.J. heard his father say. "We have an assignment in Peru."

C.J. wanted to shout in his excitement.

Roland Everett was Chief of Operations for all of Angus Kask's expeditions. C.J. liked Roland, especially when he heard Roland had flown in an airplane.

His father continued. "Can you get the Falcon ready in a week?"

The Falcon was a steamship that his father used on his expeditions. They named it after C.J.'s favorite bird. It seemed appropriate since the ship seemed to fly through the water at 22 knots.

"I know it's a short notice," Angus said. "The museum has some people who may need help. Can you get it ready?"

There was a pause as Angus listened to Roland's reply.

"Contact everyone and get back to me," His father said and hung up the telephone.

Angus returned to the living room. C.J. could not control himself in his excitement.

"Are we going?" he asked.

Angus jumped. He frowned at his son. "I thought I told you to go to bed."

"I know, but I had to find out what they wanted," C.J. said. "Are we going?"

"I don't know. Roland is checking on it."

"Have you ever been to Peru? I haven't."

"I know you haven't," his father told him. "And no, I have never been to Peru. I was in Chile, just south of it, but not Peru. Now, please, go to bed."

"I won't be able to sleep."

"Try."

C.J. nodded and went upstairs. Before he could get into bed, he heard the two short rings of the telephone, which meant the call was for them. He bounded downstairs again.

"Is that Mr. Everett?" C.J. asked.

Angus said nothing, but returned to the study.

"Hello?" C.J. heard his father ask. "Did you get a hold of everyone?"

C.J. wanted to go to Peru.

"Will the ship be ready?" his father asked.

C.J. clasped his hands together. "Please, please, please," he whispered to himself.

"I understand," his father said and hung up again.

It did not surprise Angus to see his son standing in the living room, waiting to find out if they were going.

"How many times do I have to tell you to go to bed?" his father asked.

"Once, after you tell me we're going," C.J. told him.

Angus smiled at him. Even though he didn't understand the dangers involved in some expeditions they'd been on, his son was always excited to go.

"Will you go to bed if I tell you?"

"Yes, are we going?"

Angus's smile faded. He looked at his son with a frown.

"I'm afraid..." he said and then paused.

C.J. looked at him in disbelief. Were they not going?

"I'm afraid," his father continued, "We'll have to pack our bags again. We're going to Peru."

Chapter 3

They spent several days aboard a train from Minneapolis to Chicago and then to San Francisco. When they left the train station, C.J. wandered the streets of the big city, thrilled to be off the train. During the train trip, C.J.'s father told him about the powerful earthquake that struck San Francisco in the year that he was born. He almost expected to see the city still in ruins.

They stayed at the Palace Hotel for one night. Their room was on the fifth floor, and C.J. rode in an elevator for the first time. He was a little scared when the door closed on the little room, but he tried not to show it. However, when they arrived on their floor, C.J. wanted to return to the lobby and ride it up again.

C.J. stepped out of the motorized cab at the dock the following day. He gazed up in wonder at the Falcon. He had only been on the ship one other time and couldn't wait to sail on it again.

The ship was a 135-foot wood-hulled steam yacht built for speed but with some comforts for long expeditions to far-off lands. It had a pair of smokestacks for its steam engines and two masts so that it could still run on sails.

Many of the twelve-member crew stood on deck waiting for the passengers to arrive.

Roland Everett was on the dock at the bottom of the gangplank. The man was tall, taller than C.J.'s father. He had dark hair and always seemed to have a deep tan. The man reminded C.J. of the wrestlers he'd seen at county fairs that would challenge anyone to a match.

"Is everyone on board?" Angus asked him.

"No, just the Halls," Roland said.

Angus nodded. He and C.J. grabbed their bags and headed up onto the ship. Captain Thomas Jacobs greeted them and welcomed them aboard.

A member of the crew directed them to the cabins. They followed the deck until they came to the doors of the main saloon. C.J. stared at the smokestacks and masts that towered above them.

His foot slipped on a board that was wet and fell forward. He dropped his bags as he stumbled and would have fallen face-first into the wood deck if the crewman hadn't grabbed and steadied him back on his feet.

"Are you all right, sir?" the man asked after C.J. had recovered.

"I guess so," C.J. told him. He had never been called 'sir' before.

"I think he'll be fine," C.J.'s father said. "You'll have to watch your footing," he told C.J. "It'll be worse when we're out at sea. You don't want to end up in the ocean."

C.J. nodded. He grabbed his bags again and followed his father into the saloon.

The saloon was a large open room where the passengers could gather, and, with Angus Kask's expeditions, they could discuss plans. Three people were waiting for them.

Jackson and Teresa Hall were members of the expedition and experts in anthropology. Their daughter, Laura, was a year younger than C.J. and was sitting in a corner reading a book, as usual. C.J. suspected that it was a book about some ancient dead language.

He waved at Laura, who had looked up from her book when they entered the saloon. She waved back and went right back to reading.

After they greeted the elder Halls, C.J. and his father went below to settle into their cabin.

By the time C.J. returned to the saloon, more people had arrived. Edna MacGregor, the team's botanist, and Walter MacGregor, an archaeologist, were chatting with the Halls. Their son, ten-year-old Scotty MacGregor, was sitting beside Laura.

Scotty called C.J. over. "Isn't it great? We're going to Peru," Scotty said. "Think of it. The Inca were master masons, you know."

C.J. didn't know, but it wasn't a surprise that Scotty did. He loved anything to do with engineering and building.

"And the roads. Did you know they built roads everywhere? And, of course, they were fantastic at making rope bridges."

"Of course," C.J. agreed. Laura and C.J. smiled at each other. They liked Scotty and his enthusiasm for the Inca accomplishments, but sometimes he didn't know when to stop.

The door to the saloon opened again and interrupted Scotty.

Axel van Housen and his son, Frederick, entered and dropped their bags. Axel chomped on a cigar as he glanced around the room at the people who had arrived before them. He was the head of security for the expedition. He was also an expert on ancient warfare and weapons.

C.J. always kept his distance from the man. Axel wasn't friendly, and C.J. didn't like him very much. C.J. especially didn't enjoy the smoke from his cigars.

Frederick was a year older than C.J. and much the same as his father. He was an excellent marksman, and C.J. respected him for that, but they were not friends.

Frederick glared at C.J., but when a red-haired girl wearing a tan shirt and khaki pants came up the stairs from the stateroom, both boys' attention went to her.

Sadie MacGregor was Scotty's sister and was the same age as C.J. Edna MacGregor shook her head when she saw how her daughter dressed, but said nothing to her.

At home, Sadie wore dresses as any proper girl of the time did. On expeditions, though, she dressed like the boys, and her mother had long since stopped trying to fight her about it.

She greeted everyone in the room with a smile and then sat down with C.J., Scotty, and Laura.

Frederick glared at C.J. again when Sadie sat down next to him. He grabbed his bags and followed his father down to their stateroom.

When they returned, everyone was present, and Angus took charge of the group. "Thank you all for coming. We will leave port soon. Please, make yourselves at home. As soon as we reach open seas, I will give you the details of the expedition."

"Can we at least know where we are going?" Axel van Housen asked.

"Of course," Angus said. "Our destination is the site of an Inca temple in the mountains near Lima, Peru. It will take us a little over a week to get there and we will need all of that time to prepare. In the meantime, if you have not already, stow your gear below and we'll get underway."

C.J.'s father was correct. It took just over a week, and the adults spent most of their time examining maps of the area and finding out everything they could about the little-known site.

The young explorers were interested in learning about Peru and the Inca civilization that flourished there over four hundred years earlier. When the Spanish Conquistadors arrived in the early 1500s, it spelled the end of the Inca Empire.

They discovered the site was south of Lima, the capital of Peru and its largest city. There was a ruined temple several miles up a mountain. The temple stood on a plateau and they dedicated it to Inti, the sun god. The sun was vital to the Inca, many of whom were farmers. It was natural that they would worship a god that represented the sun.

Everyone also learned more about the pyramid that was discovered by the original team. Angus told them he had no additional information on the pyramid since the museum lost communications after the team opened it.

When they weren't in the saloon listening to their parents' conversations, the kids played whist, except Frederick. He didn't join in games with the others, but he always seemed to be close by, especially if Sadie was there.

On the eighth day of the voyage, the captain announced they were approaching the coast of Peru. C.J. and Sadie hurried out onto the deck. They wanted to watch their progress to the port at Lima.

It was early morning, and they could see the distant coastline. They hoped they would arrive in port before too long. However, one crew member told them they wouldn't be in Lima until late afternoon.

They leaned on the railing and watched the land pass by as they headed south to Lima. They talked about the Andes that towered in the distance, poison dart frogs, and malaria, a disease that was a significant problem in the area.

Poisons, diseases, and anything else related to medicine fascinated Sadie. Often when they talked about such things, her medical jargon went over his head.

Their conversation was interrupted when Frederick pushed between them and shoved C.J. aside.

"Hey," C.J. said. "I was standing there."

"Well, now I am," Frederick said.

"Come on, C.J.," Sadie said, frowning at Frederick. "Let's go back inside."

"Good idea," Frederick said, following Sadie into the saloon.

By then, Scotty and Laura appeared at the saloon door to see what was happening outside.

"She meant me," C.J. said, "not you." He tried to push past Frederick, but Frederick held his arm out to stop him.

"You don't have to hang around us all the time," Frederick said, shoving C.J. back. "Why don't you leave us alone?"

C.J. lost his balance and stumbled backward. He almost regained his balance, but his feet slid on the slippery deck. Falling toward the railing, he tried to grab onto it, but flipped over the bar instead.

Before anyone could react, C.J. was overboard and falling toward the churning ocean below.

Chapter 4

As C.J. fell over the railing, everyone began yelling. Sadie, Scotty, and Laura ran to the rail. They looked over the side and saw C.J. hanging from the bottom rail by one hand.

Sadie slid onto the deck and braced her feet on either side of his hand. She grabbed his wrist and sleeve. She could see his fingers turning white.

"Hold on," Sadie yelled to him. She saw he was trying to reach with his other arm high enough to grab onto the rail. She yelled over her shoulder, "Someone grab his other hand!"

Despite the cool breeze, she was sweating. She felt her hand slipping down his, and she was afraid that if she lost his hand, the sleeve she held would rip away, and he would be gone.

She heard a commotion behind her as the adults poured out onto the deck. In a moment, Angus and Roland were beside her. They reached over and grabbed the boy by his arms and hauled him up and over the railing. They set him on the deck, where he gasped for breath. His whole body was shaking.

"What happened?" Angus demanded.

Scotty and Laura began talking and gesturing wildly. Angus just shook his head. He couldn't understand what either of them was saying. After sticking two fingers in his mouth and giving a shrill whistle, the noise ended.

"One at a time," Angus told them.

"He slipped," Sadie said. Everyone turned to find her sitting against the railing. "On those wet boards there. He fell through the railing." She rubbed her hands. She said quietly, "I thought he was a goner."

Angus kneeled next to his son. "Is that what happened?" he asked.

C.J. glanced around the crowd. His eyes fell on Frederick standing behind the adults with his back against the saloon windows. His eyes darted around the group like a cornered animal looking for a way out.

"C.J.?" his dad prompted him.

C.J. looked at his father. "Yes. We were looking out at the mountains and I slipped on the deck." He glanced up at Frederick. "It was an accident."

Angus saw C.J.'s glance and said nothing for a minute. Then he said, "Ok, are you all right?"

"I think so," C.J. said as he sat up. "My arm hurts a little, though."

"Why don't we all go back into the saloon?" Edna MacGregor suggested.

As everyone filed back inside the saloon, Frederick pulled C.J. aside.

"Why didn't you tell?" Frederick asked.

"Because it's between you and me," C.J. said.

"Just because you covered for me doesn't get you any brownie points," Frederick told him.

"I wasn't looking for any," C.J. said, leaving him alone on the deck.

Frederick looked out at the ocean and then followed him in. He stayed away from the other kids until they got into port.

About mid-afternoon, one crew member entered the saloon and announced they would dock shortly. C.J. and the other kids went to the saloon windows to glimpse Lima as the ship entered the harbor.

"I can't wait to be in the mountains," Scotty said.

"I hope I have time to buy an alpaca blanket," Laura said. C.J. glanced over at Frederick, who had spent most of the last couple of hours with his father. Frederick saw him and looked away.

Once they docked and the customs officials cleared them to disembark, the adults unloaded their gear onto the dock. The kids helped with what they could, but spent a lot of time looking at the multi-colored buildings along the waterfront and the Peruvians in the streets dressed in a mix of modern and traditional clothing.

"It looks so old," Frederick said.

"It is old," Laura said. "Francisco Pizarro founded it in 1535. He was a Spanish Conquistador who came to South America to conquer the Incas."

"I like San Francisco better," Frederick said.

A truck pulled around the corner and came to a noisy stop at the end of the dock. Roland jumped out and hurried over to the pile of equipment waiting to be loaded. Once all the equipment was on the truck, Angus called the kids to climb in.

Angus and Roland climbed into the cab with Roland driving. Everyone else piled into the back with the equipment. The truck had low wooden sidewalls with curved bars overhead to form a roof. A tent material covered half the top, and the rest was open to the sky.

They drove south through the city, headed for the rural area south of Lima. The kids enjoyed seeing the old buildings through the open roof of the truck as they made their way through the city. Before long, the buildings disappeared. They could only see the mountains rising on one side and the waves crashing on the other.

After over an hour, they turned inland and headed up a road into the mountains. The sun was setting when the truck came to a stop.

Roland appeared at the back gate and told them they would have to hike to the site.

They unloaded the truck, and parceled out the supplies so that everyone, even the kids, was carrying their fair share of the load. Once that was done, they climbed the mountain along a rough path.

The sky was darkening, and several people brought out lanterns to light their way. The kids saw the mountainside didn't slope down evenly. It had giant steps carved into the mountain, worn away in some places and overgrown everywhere else.

Teresa Hall saw them looking at the steps. "Those were terraces that the Inca used to grow the food they needed. You can't farm on a slope, so they cut steps into the mountainside."

After what seemed like hundreds of miles to the kids, they reached the top of the slope and passed several rectangles of broken rock.

"What are they?" C.J. asked his father.

"I'd say they were some homes or storehouses. Farmers and shepherds used to live up here," his father told him.

At the top of the bluff, not far away, they saw the outline of a ruined building in the twilight. They had to cross a dark gully cutting down the slope.

"It looks like a dry stream bed," Angus said, peering into the gully. "When the mountain snow melts in the spring, the runoff probably comes through here," he said.

Roland pointed to an old rope bridge that crossed the narrow gap. "Hopefully that's still strong enough for us to cross," he said.

It looked strong, but they didn't take any chances. They crossed the bridge one person at a time.

"The Inca could have built this," Scotty told everyone as he crossed.

"We're here," Angus announced as the last person finished crossing.

Behind the ruins, they could see the camp. There were a few pup tents for sleeping and several larger tents used as lab spaces.

Beyond the camp, a bonfire blazed before an opening into the mountain. Someone had cleared the debris away on both sides, revealing the bottom steps of a pyramid. They could see the flicker of torchlight inside.

As they entered the camp, they realized the tents were dark, and everything was quiet.

"They don't seem to have the welcome mat out," Roland told Angus quietly.

"Seems that way," Angus said. "Well, let's see if they want to come out to play." He dropped the supplies he was carrying. "Hello," he called. "Potter? Freitag? This is Angus Kask."

After a moment, they heard movement in one of the large tents. Someone opened a flap, and two men came out. They stood facing the newcomers.

"Angus," a tall, skeletal-looking man greeted him. "We weren't expecting visitors."

"I understand," Angus said. "The museum was worried about you, Freitag."

"There was no need to be," Freitag said.

"They hadn't heard a word from you in several weeks," Angus said. "They sent me down here to make sure you were all right."

"Totally unnecessary," Freitag told him.

"Necessary or not, we're here," Angus said, "at least for the night."

The two men stood facing each other in silence. Everyone could feel the tension between the two.

The man standing next to Freitag broke the silence. "Otto," he said to Freitag, "let's be a little more gracious to our guests." He strode over to Angus and shook his hand. "Welcome, Dr. Kask. My name is Dr. Ralf Eberhardt. I am the camp physician."

"Thank you, Doctor," Angus said, glancing over the man's shoulder at Freitag, who was still standing at the tent's entrance. "We don't want to disrupt anything. All we need is a little space to set our supplies and put up some tents for the night."

Eberhardt looked to Freitag. Freitag just stared and then shrugged his shoulders. "Over there," he said, waving a hand at a flat area away from the camp.

"Thank you again, Doctor," Angus said, and the group set to prepare their camp. They lit some kerosene lamps and began putting up their tents. Angus left Roland to the preparations and returned to Freitag's camp. C.J. followed him.

Freitag was standing right where they had left him. He knew Angus would return.

"Where's Potter?" Angus asked.

"He left us," Freitag said.

"He left?"

"Yes, some weeks ago. We woke up one morning, and he just wasn't there."

"Why would he leave?" Angus asked.

"He didn't say," Freitag said. "That's why we haven't been able to send word to Chicago."

"No one else knows how to send messages?"

"I'm afraid not. We're simple men, Angus," he said. "We don't know about these technical things."

Before Angus could say anything more, a man's scream echoed across the plateau.

"Who was that?" Angus asked, glancing around.

"It was Carter," Freitag said. "He was tending the fire at the pyramid."

Angus, C.J., and Freitag ran to the pyramid. Roland, Axel, and Dr. Eberhardt joined them on the way.

At the bonfire, there was no sign of Carter.

"Where is he?" Freitag asked.

Just then, a man stumbled out of the pyramid and fell, dropping several rocks he was carrying.

"Help me," he whimpered. He reached out toward the nearest man. He was bleeding, but it was hard to tell how much because it blended into the red material of his shirt. "Please."

Angus and Eberhardt ran toward him, but something dragged the man back through the doorway and out of sight before anyone could reach him.

The men rushed to the opening. Carter was lying in the shadows several yards down a passageway. A torch burned on both sides of the entrance, and another torch sputtered in the dust, apparently where the man had dropped it.

They ran into the pyramid. Freitag and Eberhardt grabbed torches while Roland and Axel ran toward the man. Angus and C.J. stayed at the door, staring at the moving shadow in the corridor behind the man.

Carter tried to crawl back toward them. Before he could get even a yard closer, a shadowy figure moved out of the darkness of the passage behind him. It fell onto the man, covering him, and he screamed.

Roland and Axel moved to help the man, but Freitag and Eberhardt held them back.

"It's too late," Freitag said without emotion.

Axel pulled out a pistol and aimed. He shot at the figure, but it seemed to go through it. Roland drew a knife. Freitag put a hand on his arm.

"You can't help him," he said, his voice barely rising above the man's screams.

They all stared in horror as the man's face grew thin. His hair quickly turned white and fell off his head. His scream became gruff, weak, and finally died off.

The shadowy figure withdrew from the man and faded back into the darkness of the passage. The man lying on the pyramid floor was just bones, clothes, and dust.

Chapter 5

Angus kneeled down to look at the remains of the man's body. He couldn't believe that the man was alive just a few moments before. The bones looked like he had died long ago.

"Oh, my god," he said. Roland and Axel had the same reaction.

Freitag and Eberhardt stood by with torches and watched in case the creature returned.

Angus gathered the bones up in the man's clothes and carried them out of the pyramid. Several of Freitag's men were just arriving to help.

"What was that?" C.J. asked.

"A spirit," his father said.

"A wraith," Eberhardt told them. "An evil spirit. We first discovered it after we opened the pyramid."

"Where?"

"We were in a room deep inside the mountain examining the mummies that we found there. It must have been waiting for us down there in the dark. It grabbed one of our men and dragged him away."

"Did the same thing happen to him?" Angus asked.

"We don't know. We never found his body."

"The darkness," Angus said, thoughtfully. "It likes the darkness."

"We noticed it seemed to stay away from anyone who had a light source," Freitag said.

Angus nodded. "That's why you have the bonfire burning at the entrance and the torches on the walls."

"Yes," Freitag said. "As long as we have plenty of light, we seem to be safe from the creature. We set the bonfire at the entrance to prevent it from escaping into the darkness at night."

"Imagine what would happen if it got out into the world," C.J. said. He shivered at the thought.

He looked down at the rocks that the man had spilled on the ground and picked a couple up. He looked at the bigger one. It was a rough piece of quartz with black and reddish yellow veins running through it.

"What is this?" he asked.

Freitag picked one up. "I'll have them analyzed." He called to two of his men. "Gather them up and take them back to the lab." The men did as they were told.

He held out his hand to C.J. "Let's keep them all together, shall we?"

C.J. looked at the rock again and then handed it to Freitag. They added the rock to the rest and the two men hurried back to camp. C.J. slipped the smaller rock into his pocket.

"Otto," Angus said, "you didn't see what happened to the first man because it dragged him away."

"That is correct," Freitag said.

"How did you know what would happen this time?"

Freitag said nothing. C.J. noticed that all of Freitag's men stopped what they were doing and were waiting to hear what he was going to say.

"You saw another attack," Angus said.

Freitag glanced at Eberhardt. "Yes," he said. "There was another... injury."

"Injury," C.J. said. "You mean someone survived?"

"Yes," Freitag replied.

"What kind of injury?" Angus asked.

"I think it would be best if you see for yourself," Freitag said. He started down the hill toward camp. The rest of his men followed. Of Freitag's men, only Eberhardt and a man named Granville stayed back.

"Roland, you and Axel check on the rest of our group," Angus said. "We'll need to set up a watch."

Axel chomped down on his ever-present cigar and nodded. He and Roland headed off toward their camp.

"Dr. Eberhardt," Angus said, "lead the way." He and C.J. followed the doctor back to Freitag's camp. Granville stayed behind to tend the bonfire.

C.J. walked behind the two men and pulled the rock from his pocket. Freitag and his men knew something about the rocks. He looked at the colors embedded in the quartz. He wondered why they wanted the rocks?

As they entered the camp, Eberhardt stopped and talked to two men he called Jensen and Hayes. C.J. quickly slipped the rock back into his pocket before anyone could see it. After a quick word, the two men hurried back toward the pyramid.

"They're going to bring Carter's body down to the equipment tent until we decide what to do with him," Eberhardt told them as he continued on toward the largest of their tents.

"What are you going to do with him?" asked C.J.

"We could bury him here or transport him back to the States," Eberhardt said.

C.J. wasn't sure what to think about the doctor. He talked so casually about a member of his team who was alive and well just a short time before and now lay in the dirt on the hill with the life sucked out of him.

Eberhardt opened the tent flap for them, and C.J. followed his father. Inside, the tent was well lit with kerosene lamps. Workbenches and archaeological equipment lined the walls.

Papers covered a large table in the center of the tent, scattered across a diagram of the site. C.J. could see the plateau, sections of the temple ruins, and part of the foot of the pyramid.

Several people worked at the tables cleaning artifacts or drawing additional diagrams. On one table, a large bulky item lay wrapped with cloth. C.J. went over to look at it.

Freitag entered the tent from the other side. He immediately pointed out some telegraph equipment in the corner.

"Our communications equipment," Freitag said to Angus. "It's no use to us without someone who can operate it."

"Can I have one of my men use it?" Angus asked.

"If you have someone who can operate it, you are welcome to try," Freitag said.

Angus picked up a machine from the corner of the main table that comprised a pendulum hanging over a rotating drum. There was graph paper wrapped around the drum.

He looked up at Freitag. "Was Potter the man you lost in the pyramid?"

"No, that was one of our field technicians." Freitag took the device from Angus and put it on a side table.

No one was paying any attention to what C.J. was doing, so he pulled the cloth back to see what was in the large bundle. A face stared back at him. Startled, he cried out and backed away from the table, banging into a chair behind him.

"C.J., what's wrong?" Angus asked.

"He was just startled by our mascot." Freitag said and laughed for the first time. He pulled the cloth off the bundle. A mummified body lay underneath.

"What is that?" C.J. asked.

"It is the body of a young Inca boy," Freitag said, "probably nine or ten years old."

"Why did you remove him from the pyramid?" Angus asked.

"It's a curious case. We found it lying against a wall just inside the entrance," Freitag told him.

"Lying against a wall?"

"It probably wasn't dead when the door was closed," Freitag said.

"It?" C.J. asked. "Don't you mean 'he'?"

"If you prefer," Freitag said. "Either way, it could have been an accident or a punishment."

"What about this injured man you spoke of?" Angus asked.

Eberhardt pulled open a tent flap leading into another section of the tent. "This way," he said.

C.J. took one last quick look at the mummified boy and then followed his father through the tent door.

That section of the tent was the camp's infirmary. There was a small changing room between the two sections so that visitors can drop any unnecessary equipment and put on protective clothing before entering the hospital room beyond.

"Please put on these masks," Eberhardt told them. He already had one on. "We don't want the patient contaminated."

When they entered the next room, they found it contained two beds. One was empty, a mosquito netting covered the other. It was difficult to see through the netting clearly, but C.J. could make out the general form of the man lying under a sheet.

"He is in a very fragile condition," Eberhardt told them. "As you saw, the creature seems to drain all the life out of a person until they age and decay."

"I've seen nothing like it," Angus said.

"No, I don't think anyone has," Eberhardt said. "In his case, we used the light from our torches to scare the wraith away before it could kill him."

"Was he a technician too?" C.J. asked.

"No," Eberhardt said. "This is Thomas Potter."

"Freitag said Potter disappeared," Angus said.

Eberhardt shook his head. "He thought it would be difficult to understand what had happened to him. Nobody could understand this unless they had seen the creature first hand."

"And now we have," Angus said.

Eberhardt nodded. "Now you have."

"How did the wraith get him?" C.J. asked.

"After the first attack, we realized the wraith didn't like the light," Eberhardt told them. "So, whenever we went into the pyramid after that, some of us would process the artifacts, and others would stand guard with torches."

"A wise precaution," Angus said.

"We thought so," Eberhardt agreed. "Everything went well for days. There was no sign of the wraith."

"But it came back?" C.J. asked.

"Potter accidentally dropped his torch into the dirt, and it went out. There was plenty of light from other torches, but he tried to retrieve his."

"And the wraith got him," C.J. said.

"Yes," Eberhardt told them, "it got him. Several of the men converged on him and waved their torches at the creature. It gave out a shrill cry and disappeared into the darkness. It was only a matter of seconds."

"We should look at Potter," Angus said.

Eberhardt sighed. "Very well," he said. He looked at C.J. and paused a moment. "Perhaps just your father and I should look at the patient."

"I can handle it," C.J. said.

"I'll leave it up to you," Eberhardt told him.

He went to the patient's bed and pulled the mosquito netting back. Angus and C.J. crowded into the small area beside the bed.

"Don't be alarmed," Eberhardt said about the cloth over the man's face. "We cover his face with this damp gauze to keep his skin moistened. He can easily breathe through it." He paused before pulling it off. "It has the added benefit that we don't have to look at his face," he said.

When they were ready, Eberhardt removed it.

Both C.J. and his father gasped.

The man's stringy white hair barely covered the top of his emaciated head. The skin over his face was thin and seemed transparent. It gave them the impression that you could see the white of his skull through it. Even worse, his nose appeared to be decaying.

"He looks like he's more than a hundred years old," C.J. said.

"He's not," Angus said. "I knew Potter when he was just a little boy."

"You are correct, Dr. Kask," Eberhardt told them. "Thomas Potter is twenty-eight years old."

Chapter 6

When C.J., Angus, and Eberhardt left the infirmary, they found the rest of the tent crowded with people. Kask's team had gathered in the tent with most of the members of Freitag's team.

"Roland," Angus said, "check out that telegraph and see if you can get a message to Chicago."

"Right," Roland replied. "My Morse code is a little rusty, though."

Angus glanced at Freitag, who appeared impassive as always. "Just make sure it works, for now. We'll send them information later," he told Roland.

Roland sat down at the communication equipment.

"We can talk to someone in Chicago?" C.J. asked.

"We use wireless telegraphy to transmit our message to the museum's receiver in Chicago," Angus told him.

"Without wires?" C.J. asked.

"Without wires," Angus said. "It sends out electromagnetic waves through the air."

"Do you still use Morse code?"

"We do. Do you remember your Morse code?"

"Mr. Jenkins, the train station agent, let me listen to messages, and I practiced writing them down," C.J. said. "He doesn't let me send any messages, though."

"Well, maybe you can send a message for us later," Angus told him.

"That would be great," C.J. said, and then he hurried over to where the other kids had gathered. Sadie was looking at some old jars.

"What are these?" C.J. asked.

"I'm not sure," Sadie said. "They found them in the pyramid. The jars could hold what's left of a mummy's internal organs if the Incas used a process like the Egyptians."

"Yuck," C.J. said, crinkling his nose at the jars.

"Or they could just be something that the Incas considered valuable and wanted to send it with the dead into their afterlife."

"That sounds better," C.J. told her. He opened a tall one and looked into it. It looked like some kind of woven fabric rolled up inside, but C.J. didn't want to touch it in case it was fragile.

C.J. opened another jar that was shorter and wider. Two pieces of carved wood were inside. They looked like six-sided elongated pyramids. Again, he didn't want to touch them, but he could see that the sides had target-like symbols on them, a different number of symbols on each side.

"What is this?" he asked, showing them to Sadie.

"I don't know," Sadie said. "An abacus? Or dice?"

C.J. shrugged and closed the jar again. He looked at the other jars on the table, but he didn't feel like looking in any more of them. He looked around to see what everyone else was up to.

Laura was looking at something piled on a side desk. They found her carefully looking at some multi-colored, knotted cords.

"What are these?" Sadie asked.

"I think these are Khipu," Laura said.

"What?" Sadie asked.

"The Inca didn't have a written language," Laura told them. "Some believe that they used knotted cords like these for keeping track of things."

"Like how many llamas they owned?" C.J. asked.

Laura rolled her eyes at him. "It was more than that," she said. "It could be a kind of three dimensional writing."

"What do these say?" Sadie asked.

"I don't know," Laura said. "Nobody has translated the meaning of the Khipu yet."

"I'm sure you'll be the first," C.J. said.

"That would be wonderful," Laura said and went back to studying the cords.

C.J. and Sadie left Laura to her knots and went to see what Sadie's brother was up to.

They found Scotty leaning over the central table, peering at the diagrams of the temple and pyramid.

"Look at this," he told them when they came near. He pointed to an artist's rendering of a section of the temple wall. The part that still existed out on the plateau was in a darker color, and the artist filled in the missing stones with a lighter color.

"What about it?" Sadie asked.

"The Inca cut the stones for this with stone or bronze tools. Can you imagine cutting all that with those kinds of tools?" he asked them. He always spoke rapidly when he was excited about something.

"That would be tough," C.J. agreed.

"And they didn't have the wheel," Scotty said. "They rolled them on wood beams and earth ramps."

"Amazing," Sadie said with a smile.

"And even with all that against them," Scotty told them, "they constructed walls that could withstand earthquakes."

"Earthquakes?" C.J. asked.

"Yeah, the stones would vibrate, but they would stay in place so the wall wouldn't break apart. It's all in how they put the stones together. By placing a large stone just right, you could even create a wall that pivots open like a door."

"Are there any of those in the pyramid?" C.J. asked.

"Sure," Scotty said. "Maybe." He paused. "I don't know."

Roland interrupted the conversations in the room when he called out to Angus. "The wireless isn't working. We won't be able to get a message through to Chicago."

Later, in a tent that Axel and Roland had erected at their camp, the kids gathered around C.J. to hear about what had happened at the pyramid.

He told them about the attack and what Freitag had told them about the wraith. They were on the edge of their seats when they heard about the withered young man in the infirmary.

It all reminded C.J. of telling ghost stories around a campfire, trying to scare everyone. Except this was no ghost story. It was real. And it scared everyone.

"It sucked the life out of him?" Scotty asked. "What if it comes after us?"

"I think they should close up the pyramid and seal it inside," Laura said. Scotty nodded his agreement.

"We should kill it," Frederick announced. Everyone looked at him. "Send it back to where it came from."

"How do we do that?" C.J. asked. "Bullets and knives don't work against it. All it fears is light."

"Burn it then," Frederick suggested.

"We should find out more about it," Sadie said.

"It wants to kill us," C.J. said.

"It must exist for a reason," Sadie said. "It might answer questions about what happens after death."

"For once," C.J. said, "I agree with Frederick."

Despite agreeing with Frederick about the fate of the wraith, he didn't trust him. C.J. wanted to talk about the rocks, but not in front of Frederick. He wanted to talk to Sadie about it privately.

"I'm going for a walk," he announced. "Sadie, do you want to come with?"

She protested about going out in the dark with the wraith out there somewhere, but she saw that there was something important he wanted. "Just a quick walk," she said.

Frederick moved to add himself to their group. C.J. quickly cut him off. "You all stay here," he said. "We'll be back in a few minutes."

They ducked out of the tent before any of the others could respond.

C.J. led Sadie a little away from the camp so that no one could overhear their conversation. They found themselves at the base of the steps leading up to the ruined temple. The moon was almost full and cast a dim glow around the area. They sat on the steps and looked down the valley at the ocean.

"The man that died in the pyramid was carrying a bunch of rocks when it attacked him," C.J. told her. "Afterward, Freitag was quick to collect them. He got all of them except this one." C.J. pulled the rock out of his pocket. He gave it to Sadie, who studied it in the dim light.

"What do you think it is?" Sadie asked.

"I don't know," he said. "It was important to Freitag to get them before we could look at them closely."

Sadie handed it back. He put it back in his pocket.

He was going to say something more about the rock when he heard Sadie gasp. He looked up at her. She was staring at the edge of the bluff. C.J. turned to look. He saw nothing at first, but then something moved in the dark, like a shadow.

They stood and backed away quickly. As the shadow moved into the light of the moon, they saw it was a black dog.

"Is that the wraith?" Sadie asked. She seemed ready to flee.

"I don't think so. The wraith looked more like a man," C.J. told her, but he too was ready to run if the dog came at them.

Sadie fumbled for something she had in her pocket. She found it and held it out for the dog. It was a piece of jerky. C.J. remembered that he had some, too. They all did. It was something easy to carry on expeditions and didn't spoil.

The dog approached them and sniffed at the jerky, but didn't take it. It sat down out of their reach.

C.J. kneeled down and reached his hand out toward the dog with his fingers loosely curled under, encouraging the dog to get to know him. The dog leaned forward and, after a quick sniff of the back of his hand, sat upright again.

"It doesn't have a collar," Sadie said. "Do you think it belongs to someone at the camp?"

"Maybe," C.J. said. "It doesn't seem wild. It could belong to a farmer around here."

All three of them jumped at the sound of a log being thrown onto the bonfire. C.J. and Sadie turned their attention to the fire for a moment. When they looked back, the dog was running off into the darkness.

"What kind of dog?" Scotty asked when C.J. and Sadie returned and told them what had happened.

"I don't know," C.J. said.

"Maybe it belongs to the others," Scotty said. "I hope so. It would be fun to have a dog around. I've always wanted a dog. Haven't I, Sis?" he asked Sadie. She nodded.

"You shouldn't be out at night," Laura told them. "It could have been the wraith."

"I'll go with you next time," Frederick announced. "I'd protect you from danger." He held up a spear.

"If you had killed that dog," Sadie told him, "I would never have spoken to you again."

"Why don't we calm down and relax?" C.J. asked. "Anyone want to play Whist?"

Everyone but Frederick wanted to play.

Frederick tried to ignore the rest. He checked out some equipment that the adults had unloaded. He noticed a metal box frame with wires and a battery inside. On a metal panel, there were switches and dials.

"What is this?" he asked.

"That's a radio receiver," Scotty said. "I've been working on it whenever there is nothing else to do."

"A what?" Frederick asked.

"A radio receiver," Scotty repeated, "like the wireless telegraph, except it only receives a signal."

"You can't send?" Frederick asked. "What good is it if you can't send a signal?"

"Some people have been experimenting with transmitting voice and music over wireless. Someday everyone will have one of these," Scotty told him.

"Does it work?" Frederick asked.

"I think it's working, but I don't know for sure," Scotty said.

"Why not?" Frederick asked.

"There's no signal to pick up yet," Scotty said. The others laughed.

Frederick flipped the switch, and a light turned on to show that the receiver was active. They heard static over the speaker.

"That's what you get when there isn't a signal," Scotty said. "You can turn the dial there to listen to a whole range of frequencies."

Frederick turned the dial looking for something, anything, to pick up.

The others drew cards to determine partners, and it thrilled Scotty that his partner was Laura. They took their places with C.J. and Sadie as opposing partners. Sadie dealt the hands, and the game started.

After a few hands, a rapidly beeping sound replaced the static coming from Scotty's receiver, interrupting their game.

"What is that?" Frederick asked.

"That's Morse code," C.J. said. The sounds of dots and dashes were clear and strong.

"From the strength, it must be coming from someplace close," Scotty said.

"I thought Roland said the transmitter didn't work," Sadie said.

"He did," C.J. said. "Somebody has one that works, and they probably didn't want us to know about it."

Chapter 7

The five young explorers listened to the dots and dashes of the signal on Scotty's homemade radio.

"How do we know what it says?" Scotty asked.

"It's Morse code. I think I can translate it," C.J. said. He grabbed some paper and a pencil from the table and sat down to decode the signal. As the others watched, he wrote out the letters of the message, one by one.

"What does it say?" Scotty asked, trying to look over C.J.'s shoulder.

"It looks like gibberish to me," Frederick said.

"Shush," C.J. snapped at them and continued to write the message.

"I think we should tell our parents about this," Sadie said quietly to the others.

"I'll go get them," Laura said.

"Be careful outside," Sadie told her.

"I'll go with her," Scotty said. "I'll keep her safe."

Laura shook her head, but Sadie said, "Good idea, Scotty. Now, both of you hurry."

Laura gave Sadie a dirty look and headed for the tent flap, with Scotty following behind. In a moment, they were out into the darkness, heading for the original expedition's camp.

Sadie and Frederick turned back to C.J. He had filled one sheet of paper with his large scrawl and had the next one half full. He was writing furiously.

Then suddenly, the signal stopped. They all looked at Scotty's radio.

"Was that it?" Sadie said.

"Sometimes they repeat the signal," C.J. said, "to make sure the receiver gets the message correct."

"How will we know if they repeat it?" Sadie asked.

As if in answer, the dots and dashes began again. C.J. drew a line signaling the end of the message and wrote the beginning of the new message below it.

He kept writing until the signal stopped again. He looked back at the first message and compared them.

"Yes," C.J. said. "See here? This is where I picked up the message for the first time. The rest is a repeat."

Sadie and Frederick looked at the sheets of paper. Although they couldn't understand the words, they saw it repeated.

"That's not English," Sadie said. "What language is it?"

None of the three recognized the language, although that was not surprising. None of them knew any foreign languages. C.J. knew a smattering of Spanish, but that was it.

Laura and Scotty rushed into the tent.

"We told them about the message," Scotty said. "They are on their way."

"Laura," Sadie said, "look at the message. Can you tell what language it is?"

Laura picked up the papers and glanced through them. "It is definitely German," she told them. "I know some German, but I'm not terribly fluent. My mom is, though."

"German?" Scotty said. "Freitag is German."

"So is Dr. Eberhardt," Sadie said.

"Yes, but Freitag acts like he's trying to hide something," Scotty said. "I'd bet that he's the one."

"Who's the one?" Angus Kask asked. He and the other adult members of the group entered the tent.

"Freitag," C.J. said. "Scotty thinks he was the one sending the signal."

"What signal?" Angus asked.

C.J. filled them in on Scotty's radio receiver and hearing the message in Morse code. He showed his father the pages filled with the decoded message. He ended with, "Laura thinks it's in German."

"And because it's German, that means Freitag is involved?" Angus asked.

"I think he's hiding something," Scotty said.

"Why don't we see what the message says first," Angus suggested and gave the paper to Teresa Hall, who sat down with her daughter, Laura, to translate the message.

Walter MacGregor looked at the radio receiver. "You made this, Scotty?"

Scotty smiled and nodded.

"And you could pick up a wireless telegraph signal on it?" MacGregor asked C.J.

"Loud and clear," C.J. told him.

"Good work, Scotty," MacGregor said.

Everyone sat down to wait for Teresa and Laura to finish their translation. Everyone in the Hall family was talented with languages. Laura spent most of her eleven years living in one country after another. She spoke four languages and could recognize enough phrases to get by in two or three more.

Finally, they finished their translation and checked over their work. Everyone was eager to hear the message.

Teresa stood up. "The message was in German," she said. "I'll let Laura read it to you since she did most of the translating."

Laura barely contained her excitement as she stood up to read the message.

She cleared her throat and read.

General Felix Graber, Berlin, Germany.

Arrival of a hostile group. Operation temporarily shut down. Acquired less than a quarter of the shipment prior to arrival. Abandon, wait, or eliminate hostiles?

- Raven.

"Eliminate hostiles?" C.J. repeated.

"I told you they're hiding something," Scotty said.

"Somebody is," Angus said. "We don't know who's involved."

"This Raven is not too happy we're here," Axel said. "We have to be careful."

"We can't trust any of them," Roland said. "We need to watch our backs."

"Tomorrow," Angus said. "I want all of you, except Roland and Axel, to pack up and head back down. Take the truck back to the ship. Walter, you can bring the truck back to the pickup point. By that time, the three of us should be ready to go."

"What are you going to do?" Walter asked.

"Whatever they are doing," Angus said, "it has something to do with the pyramid. They broke off communications after they opened the tomb. There is something in there they don't want anyone else to know about."

"And we're going to find out what it is," Roland said, finishing the thought.

"Do you think it is the rocks that man was carrying out of the pyramid?" C.J. asked.

"I don't know," his dad told him. "Too bad we don't have one to check out ourselves."

"I do," C.J. said.

"What?" Angus asked.

"I took one. I picked up two after the man dropped them, and when Freitag asked for the rocks back, I just gave him one." C.J. pulled the rock from his pocket and gave it to his father.

"Well done, C.J.," his father told him. He looked at the rock and frowned. "I can't see that they would go through all this cloak and dagger for a rock."

"Jackson," he called, "see what you can find out about this." He tossed the rock to the man.

Jackson looked at the rock and nodded. "I'll check it out." He pulled out some tools.

Angus turned to Roland and Axel. "We'll have to make it look like we left with the others."

"It will be harder to sneak back during the day," Axel told him.

"I know," Angus said, "but if we tried packing up and heading out at night, they would be suspicious. They want us to leave. Let's give them what they want and maybe that will put them off their guard."

"They may try to kill us," Roland said.

"According to that message, they might try to do that anyway," Angus said. "The problem is they aren't the only ones to worry about. The wraith might try to kill us, too."

"I want to go with you, Dad," C.J. told his father.

The young explorers volunteered one by one.

"No," Angus said, "I will not risk your lives. We have enough to worry about without having to worry about the five of you, too."

The five kids voiced their disappointment.

"Right now," Angus said, "the best thing you can do for us is to go to bed and get some sleep."

"I don't like the idea of them sleeping in the small tents tonight," Edna MacGregor said.

"Bring their blankets here," Walter said.

"That's a good idea," Angus said. To the kids, he said, "Get your blankets and come right back here."

They were quickly out of the main tent and headed to their own tents to gather their things.

"You three need to get some rest, too," Edna told Angus. "Walter and I will stay up and stand guard."

"Thank you, Edna," Angus told her. "Monitor Scotty's radio receiver too. We want to know if they get a reply to their message."

"Will do," Edna told him.

It wasn't long before the kids returned and settled down for the night.

Jackson brought the rock back to Angus. "I don't have the right equipment to test it," he told Angus. "But it seems to have some signs of gold. I'm not sure how much or how pure, but there is gold in it."

"Gold would explain why they are so secretive," Roland said. "If they thought they could turn the pyramid into their own private gold mine, I can see why they aren't happy we're here."

"It's an excellent cover," Angus said. "Conducting an archaeological survey and plunder the gold out of a mountain at the same time."

"Except the cover doesn't work if more archaeologists show up," Axel said.

"Exactly," Angus said. He gave the rock back to C.J. "Good work," he told him.

Once the kids were asleep, Angus, Roland and Axel sat down and planned their entry into the pyramid. Although it was a little more dangerous at night, they planned to bring several kerosene lanterns. They hoped the bright light from the lanterns would keep the creature at bay.

Finally, when the planning was done, Angus said, "Let's get some sleep. We'll need all the rest we can get if we're going into the pyramid in the morning."

The others agreed, and soon the three of them were fast asleep under the watch of Walter and Edna.

C.J. had been pretending to sleep and listened to their plan. He agreed with them on one thing. He'd need all the rest he could get because in the morning, he was going into the pyramid with them.

Chapter 8

C.J. woke to the sounds of packing. The adults were already up and breaking camp. One-by-one, the young explorers rolled out of their blankets and sleepily got ready for the day. The MacGregors prepared each of them a pancake and a few slices of bacon, after which they pitched in to help pack up.

As the main tent came down, Freitag and Eberhardt stopped over to talk with C.J.'s father.

"Leaving?" Freitag asked.

"The museum sent us down to see what happened to you," Angus told him. "We've accomplished that."

"I'm sorry to see you go," Eberhardt said. "I'm glad to have met all of you."

"It's for the best," Freitag said. "We can get back to our work." He turned and walked away.

Eberhardt looked as if he wanted to say something more, but just waved a hand and followed Freitag back to the other camp.

C.J. kept an eye on Freitag as they finished packing up. As Freitag and Eberhardt reached the main tent, two of Freitag's men, Granville and Hayes, came out and the four men spoke briefly. Freitag and Eberhardt went into the tent and left the two men outside to watch them.

After packing everything, they all picked up their backpacks. With one last look back at the original camp, they crossed the rope bridge and started down the valley path.

The two men followed behind and monitored the group. When they reached the edge of the plateau, the men stopped and watched them as they made their way down the side of the mountain.

C.J. hurried to catch up to his father. "They're watching us," he said.

"I know," Angus said without looking back.

"I want to go back with you," C.J. told his father.

Sadie added, "I do too."

"Do you?" Angus asked.

"I can be your lookout," the boy said. "I can watch their camp and warn you if they come out."

"I appreciate the offer, C.J.," his father told him, "but I think you'll be safer back on the ship."

C.J. was quiet for several minutes. Then he said, "I suppose I can catch up on my sleep. I didn't sleep well last night."

Sadie yawned. "Neither did I," she said.

"That sounds like a good idea," Angus said.

When they arrived at the truck, everyone packed their supplies into it, and the five kids climbed in.

The adults gathered in front of the truck to watch the two men up on the plateau. They hadn't moved.

Roland suggested that they all get in the truck and start driving away. At the first bend in the road that is protected from sight by trees, the three men would jump out and make their way back up the slope. Angus and Axel agreed with the plan, and they all loaded up into the truck.

When Angus climbed up into the back, he only saw three kids.

"Where's C.J. and Sadie?" he asked.

Laura looked up from her book and pointed to two figures curled up under blankets among the supplies.

"I guess they were tired," Angus said. Roland and Axel laughed.

It wasn't long before the three men got their chance. As the road curved behind some trees, Walter slowed down, and the three men slipped off the back of the truck. They hurried into the shelter of the trees and started back up the slope.

They followed the trees until they were about a hundred yards away from the top. They crept to the edge of the trees and peered up at the plateau. The two men were gone. Satisfied that no one could see them from the camp, the three men hurried up the slope to the temple ruins.

C.J. and Sadie hid in the trees just below the pyramid and saw the three men climb to the temple. They had enlisted the aid of their friends to make it look like they were sleeping in the truck while they hid in the tall grass nearby.

When the truck drove off, they watched until the men on the ridge went back to camp. Then they dashed across the road into the trees and made their way to a spot below the pyramid, just in time to see the three men emerge from the forest.

Once the men had disappeared into the temple ruins, C.J. and Sadie climbed up the embankment to the edge of the plateau.

Angus and Roland watched the pyramid from behind one end of a low wall of the temple ruins. Axel watched the camp from the other end. The only person in sight was a single guard who sat tending the bonfire in front of the pyramid.

They were discussing several ways to distract the guard when he suddenly stood and looked around. They quickly flattened themselves against the wall and waited.

"Did you think he saw us?" Angus asked.

Roland peeked over the wall. The guard hurried around the corner of the pyramid to a spot behind some rocks.

"Bathroom break," Roland laughed quietly.

They signaled to Axel, and the three of them ran across the plateau and through the entrance into the Inca pyramid.

C.J. and Sadie saw the guard disappear around the corner and the three men dash across the plateau and into the pyramid.

"Let's go," C.J. whispered to Sadie, "before the guard comes back."

They pulled themselves up onto the bluff and ran toward the pyramid. They were almost there when C.J. stumbled over an outcropping of rock and fell face down into the dirt. Sadie grabbed his arm and helped him up. Then they dashed to the pyramid entrance.

They disappeared inside just as the guard came around the corner, buttoning up his pants. He returned to his place by the fire and continued his duties.

Sadie lit a lantern they brought with them and headed down the passage into the pyramid. They followed the sounds of the three men ahead of them.

As they passed dark passages leading off to the side, Sadie glanced down at each. "It could be anywhere," she whispered to C.J.

"I know," C.J. said, "and we only brought one lantern." He had been checking the shadows all around them, too.

They came to a small room with a passage leading off to the left and stone steps leading down to the right. They stopped and listened.

"I don't hear them," Sadie said.

C.J. kneeled down and checked the tracks that crisscrossed the dirt and dust of the passageway. "Most of the tracks go toward the steps," he said, "including the most recent ones."

They descended the steps until it opened up into another small room. Even though the steps continued down, they didn't go further that way.

There was a door at the far end of the room. It stood open and light moved around inside the room beyond. The two young explorers crept up to the door and peered into it.

The room was large, with many long stone blocks lined up throughout. The Inca had hollowed out the blocks to create a kind of bowl shape and in each of these bowls contained a cloth wrapped mummy. Placed around the mummies were objects considered important to them for the afterlife.

At the other end of the room, someone had broken the stone wall, exposing the rock behind it. The light from the lanterns reflected off the rock, which looked much like the rock C.J. had picked up the day before.

Leaning against the wall were several pickaxes, a pair of wheelbarrows and a wooden crate with its lid leaning against it. It looked as if they were mining the rocks out of the mountain behind the back wall.

Freitag's group had set several lanterns around the room, but there was no sign of his men. They had just entered the room and were walking toward the first lantern when Axel leapt out at them from behind a sarcophagus. He had his rifle pointed at them, but then relaxed and lowered it.

"What are you doing?" He asked.

Angus and Roland came out of hiding. "Yes," Angus said, "what are you doing here?"

C.J. ignored their questions and changed the topic. "Is that where they got the rocks?" he asked, pointing to the far wall.

"Yes, they're digging them out of there," his father said. "Now, tell me, what are you doing here?"

"That can wait," Roland said. "We need to find out more information and get out of here before they discover us."

"I would say that it is too late for that," a voice said from the door.

Everyone spun around to find Freitag and several of his men standing there with pistols drawn.

"Now, maybe you can answer your own question, Angus," Freitag said. "What are you doing here?"

The three men quickly assessed their situation. Roland and Axel each had a weapon. Angus and the two kids did not. Freitag's men spread out by the door, cutting off the only exit from the room.

Freitag had them outnumbered and outgunned.

"We were wondering what you were up to, Otto," Angus said. "Our arrival upset you, and obviously, you were hiding something. We wanted to know what it was."

"And what did you find out?" Freitag asked.

"You turned this archaeological site into your own personal mine. What's in the rocks, Otto? What makes them so valuable?"

"That is not your concern," Freitag said.

"You didn't just stumble on it," Angus said. "You knew it was here. How?"

"You think you're the smart one," Freitag said. "Can't you figure it out?"

Angus thought about it. "A seismograph," he said. "I saw one on the table in your tent last night. You set off charges and measured the vibration with the seismograph. The variations in amplitude as it goes through different types of rock would point you in the right direction."

Freitag said nothing.

Axel lit a match. Everyone jumped at the sound.

C.J. glanced around at Freitag's men, but none of them started shooting. Axel was raising the match to a cigar that stuck out through his fingers.

"Mind if I smoke?" Axel asked.

C.J. saw something else in Axel's hand. He held two small round objects in his palm next to the cigar. C.J. recognized them as smoke bombs. Axel lit the cigar.

"You can't hold us here," C.J. shouted, trying to divert the attention away from Axel. "The others on the ship will call for help if we don't come back in time."

"Down!" Axel yelled and tossed the smoke bombs.

They each dove behind the nearest sarcophagus.

There were two minor explosions and two clouds of smoke filled the room.

C.J. and Sadie crawled out from behind the sarcophagus toward the door. They quickly made their way between the blocks of stone, being careful to avoid Freitag's men as they stumbled around the smoke-filled room.

Suddenly, a dark shape flew past C.J. and brushed his arm. He felt a chill freeze envelop his shoulder. He grabbed Sadie's arm. "The wraith," he said.

He stood and shouted to the others, "The wraith is in the room! Get the lanterns!"

He pulled Sadie to her feet and raced toward the door. When they passed a lantern on the floor, he grabbed it as they went by. The door was unguarded, and they raced through into the small room outside. They turned around and shone their lantern toward the door.

They heard a scream and some shots. Then Angus, Axel, and Roland ran out of the smoke-filled room. "Go!" Angus yelled to them. "Up the stairs."

They ran up the stairs with the men close behind. As C.J. and Sadie reached the top of the stairs, they heard Roland shout.

"Angus," he said, "watch out!"

C.J. looked back down the stairs. A dark shadowy form came at Angus rapidly from behind and knocked him to the floor. C.J. screamed as the creature fell on his father.

Chapter 9

As the wraith fell on him, Angus screamed. C.J. rushed forward to help him, but Roland grabbed him and held the struggling boy back.

"Get away from my father!" C.J. yelled at the wraith.

The wraith pulled away from the man. It floated over the steps and didn't move. Axel moved up and stood next to Angus. He held his lantern ready.

Angus lay on the steps, unconscious, his hair slightly grayer and his features gaunter, but he hadn't aged severely under the wraith's attack.

C.J. stopped struggling and Roland's grip eased. The boy pulled away and moved closer to his father, keeping his eyes on the wraith.

The wraith changed. The misty form shrank and solidified. The shadow lightened. C.J. blinked to make sure what he was seeing was actually happening.

Soon, the dark shadowy form was gone, replaced with that of a young Inca boy. The boy's image was semi-transparent, and he still floated above the steps, but there was a face that looked at them curiously.

The boy looked down at the man lying on the steps and then at C.J. He floated down toward Angus and C.J. Axel moved closer to C.J. and kept his lantern in front of him.

The boy floated toward C.J. Axel and Roland jumped between them and held their lanterns out. The boy, startled by the sudden movement, retreated down the steps until the darkness below them partially obscured him.

Axel and Roland took a step toward Angus. The image of the boy faded into the shadowy wraith form.

They raised the lanterns toward the wraith. C.J. pushed between them and waved for them to stop. The two men stopped where they were and, without quite knowing why, did what C.J. asked.

C.J. stepped up to his father and kneeled beside him. Keeping his eyes on the shadowy form, he placed his hand on his chest over his heart and tapped twice. He then moved and placed his hand over his father's heart and tapped on his chest twice.

After he repeated that again, the wraith changed back into the Inca boy. The boy nodded to C.J. and then pointed up the stairs toward the pyramid exit.

C.J. nodded and then, without turning, he said, "Roland, Axel, please carry my dad out."

The two men quickly moved to do what he asked. Sadie went to C.J. and grabbed his arm. She pulled on his arm to get him to stand up and go up the stairs.

Before the two men could pick up the unconscious man, they heard the noise of men approaching from below, and lanterns lit up the area behind the Inca boy.

The image of the boy expanded and faded as it changed back into the shadowy form of the wraith. It flew up the stairs between Axel and Roland. C.J. and Sadie ducked as it went past them. They lost sight of it as it disappeared into the darkness of a side passage and was gone.

C.J. turned back to the men approaching from below. Freitag and his men appeared below them on the steps. They had their weapons drawn.

"Don't move," Freitag told them.

They all stood where they were.

"Drop your weapons, gentlemen," Freitag ordered.

Axel laid his rifle on a step. Roland did the same.

When the weapons were safely out of reach, Freitag allowed Axel and Roland to pull Angus up into the room at the top of the stairs and lay him on the floor.

"The wraith attacked my dad," C.J. told him. "He needs a doctor."

Freitag looked down at Angus. "Interesting," he said. "Slightly gray and a little thin, but not too bad off, I think." He turned to the rest of the group. "What scared it off?"

C.J. looked down at his feet and said nothing to the man.

"We did." Roland indicated Axel and himself.

Freitag nodded but stared at C.J. curiously.

"He needs medical attention," Sadie said.

"When we get back to camp, I'll have Dr. Eberhardt check him," Freitag said. "You two," he pointed at Roland and Axel, "pick him up and carry him out." He turned to the kids. "You follow them."

Roland and Axel hesitated.

Freitag motioned to his men, who aimed their weapons at the pair. "Pick him up," he repeated.

They pulled Angus up and supported his limp body between them. After a glance back at the men who were pointing their pistols at them, they started off up the passageway toward the pyramid's entrance.

One of Freitag's men waved his gun at C.J. and Sadie. They glared at Freitag and then turned and followed the others toward the pyramid entrance.

They made their way out of the pyramid into the bright sunlight.

"I'm glad to be out of that accursed place," one of Freitag's men said. C.J. remembered that the man's name was Palmer.

"Shut up," Freitag told him.

They marched the prisoners across the plateau to their camp. The men supporting Angus stopped because they didn't know where Freitag wanted them to go. Freitag opened the flap on the main tent for them.

Once the five prisoners were in the tent, Freitag stopped Granville and Hayes. "Go check the area. Make sure the others didn't come back with them," he told them. They went to carry out their orders.

"Take him to the infirmary," Freitag said.

Palmer and Jensen nodded and waved them toward the infirmary with their guns.

"And then tie up the other four," Freitag added.

Freitag stayed behind while the two men herded their prisoners into the infirmary. Jensen told Roland and Axel to place Angus in the empty bed.

"Put your hands on your heads," Palmer ordered when they were done. The four prisoners obeyed.

While Palmer held his gun on them, Jensen tied Axel to a chair and then Roland. Once they secured the two men, the two guards seemed to relax. They tied the two kids to chairs as well.

Both men stood guard over the prisoners and kept their pistols in their hands.

Sadie glanced over at C.J. He was staring straight ahead, concentrating on something. She looked in the direction that he was looking. She couldn't see anything. What was he doing?

After some time, Palmer spoke quietly to Jensen.

"Think we should strap him down, just in case?" he asked about the unconscious man.

The other man agreed and went about securing Angus to the bed. Once he had secured the stricken man, they went back to their silent watch.

When Eberhardt entered the infirmary ten minutes later, he seemed surprised to see the four people tied to the chairs.

"Why are they tied up?" he asked them.

"Freitag's orders," Jensen told him.

He shook his head sadly and then went to Angus. They watched him check his vital signs and shine a light into his eyes. He took a blood sample and then placed a needle in his arm and connected a tube between the needle and a bag that hung from a hook over the bed.

Once he finished, he turned to the four prisoners.

"Apart from the sudden loss of energy to the creature, he is in pretty good shape," Eberhardt told them.

"What are you doing to him?" Roland asked.

"Him?" Eberhardt asked. "I'm treating him."

"What's hooked into his arm?" Roland asked.

"Oh," Eberhardt said. "I see. I am giving him a saline solution intravenously. He's dehydrated, and this is replacing the fluids that he lost."

Roland looked at him without understanding.

"I understand your confusion," Eberhardt said. "This therapy is still very new, but I assure you it's perfectly safe." He shook his head at the four of them. "You really should not have come back."

"You can't hold us here. If we don't return to the ship by nightfall, the others will summon help," Roland told him.

"By the time help can arrive, they will not find you here," Eberhardt told them. "We will be shocked, of course, that you are missing."

"How will you explain it?" Roland asked.

"We have no idea what happened to you," Eberhardt said. "Remember, you left early this morning. That's the last we saw you."

"The rest of our group knows we came back here," Axel said.

"As far as we know, you were never here," Eberhardt said. "I'm sorry, there's nothing I can do."

"Freitag is out of his mind," Roland said. "You don't have to do this."

Eberhardt narrowed his eyes at him and was silent for a moment. Then he shook his head again. "I'm sorry. I can't help you. It is out of my hands."

He turned to leave. When he reached the tent flap, he turned to the guards.

"Come with me for a moment," he said and stepped out into the infirmary entry. The two guards followed him.

As soon as the guards were out of sight, C.J. let out his breath and gasped for air. He began struggling with the ropes that bound him to the chair and was free within moments.

"How did you do that?" Sadie whispered.

"I held my breath and breathed shallow breaths," he told her as he went to work untying Roland. "I tensed my muscles. Anything to make my body take up more space."

"So when you relaxed..." Sadie started.

"The ropes would be loose, and I could get out of them," C.J. finished the sentence and untying Roland.

While Roland went to work untying Axel, C.J. untied Sadie and then hurried to the tent flap to check on Eberhardt and the guards.

He heard Eberhardt outside talking to the guards.

"I don't care what Freitag said," Eberhardt was saying. "He's in charge of the dig, but I'm in charge of this operation."

"What do you want us to do?" Jensen asked.

"I haven't received instructions on what to do with them yet," Eberhardt said. "General Graber might want a talk with Dr. Kask. So, just hold them here until we find out."

"And what if they try to escape?" Palmer asked.

Eberhardt paused, considering that possibility. Then he said, "Then shoot them all."

Chapter 10

C.J. hurried over to Roland.

"Dr. Eberhardt sent that message," he whispered. "He said that he's in charge."

"That explains why he wouldn't help us," Roland said. "Freitag wasn't calling the shots."

"He said to shoot us if we try to escape," C.J. said.

"They'll do that either way eventually," Axel said.

"We need to get Angus and find someplace safe to hide," Roland told the others. He and Axel went to work unstrapping Angus while C.J. went back to the tent flap to listen for the guards to return.

"They compromised our mission," Eberhardt was saying. "We have to get what we can and clear out."

"How long do we have?" Freitag asked. He had come back while C.J. was talking with the others.

"We have to leave tonight," Eberhardt told him. To the guards, he said, "Watch them."

C.J. rushed over to the others. "They're coming."

It was only a few moments before the tent flap opened. The two guards entered the infirmary. They looked at the chairs and froze. Ropes lay everywhere, and the chairs were empty.

They drew their guns and searched the room. Angus Kask was no longer strapped to the bed. The only person in the room was the old man in the other bed. The prisoners had escaped.

Jensen ran to summon help. Eberhardt and Freitag rushed into the infirmary. They found Palmer holding open a section of tent wall the prisoners had slashed with a knife.

"They got out here," he told them.

"Find them," Eberhardt snapped at them. "They must not escape."

The two guards ducked through the hole while Eberhardt and Freitag went back into the lab. They repeated their orders to Granville and Hayes, and soon everyone was looking for the escapees.

The men fanned out across the plateau. Palmer peered down the mountainside. There was no sign of them trying to escape to the road.

Freitag and Eberhardt checked the tents to make sure they hadn't taken refuge in one of them. Granville and Hayes searched the temple ruins while Jensen checked the pyramid.

Eberhardt and Freitag shouted for reports. One man after another reported back negatively. There was no sign of the prisoners.

"Keep looking until you have found them," Eberhardt yelled.

Granville and Hayes circled around the rock walls of the temple ruin, looking for ways into it. They climbed the broken stairs up to the remains of the entrance. The pillars that once formed the entrance had long since fallen over with the roof above collapsed down on top of it.

They looked over the debris. There was a secluded area beyond the columns where the stones that made up the temple entrance had fallen.

They kept their weapons ready as they scanned the area for any signs of life. Except for a rough statue of some Inca god and low mounds of rock and dirt, the place was empty. Granville shook his head at Hayes, and they went down the steps again to look in other nooks and crannies.

When the searchers' footsteps on the steps died away, Axel peered over the statue to make sure both of them had gone. He then went to a mound and helped Roland shake off the debris that they had piled on him earlier. One by one, he went to three more mounds and uncovered C.J., Sadie, and Angus.

Roland went to the pillars and looked out across the plateau to check on the search.

"Any ideas?" Axel asked when he joined him.

Roland just shook his head.

"The only way out is down the slope to the trees," Roland said. "If we can get to the trees, we might hide out until Walter comes back at dusk."

"They're monitoring the trees," Axel said, pointing out two of the men walking along the edge of the plateau. "There's no way we can make it with two kids and carrying Angus."

"We can't stay here," Roland said. "Eventually, they'll be back to search again."

The two men fell silent and continued their watch for some way out of their predicament.

C.J. and Sadie sat back away from the pillars in the shadows of a wall that had once been inside the temple. C.J. looked at his unconscious father.

"I wish I knew what to do," C.J. said quietly.

"None of us know what to do," Sadie told him.

"My dad would."

"Maybe, but right now, he can't help us. We have to rely on ourselves."

"We're just kids. What do we know?" C.J. asked.

"We know lots of things. We're always learning in school and from our parents," Sadie told him.

"What good is any of that?"

"You never know what might help you. The more you know, the more you have to draw on to help you out of trouble."

"Do you have any ideas?" he asked. "I know I don't." He got up and stomped off through the sand. Sadie just watched him go. He sat against the back wall by himself.

Out on the plateau, Freitag and Eberhardt took over coordinating the search. They replaced the chaos of the initial search with a systematic and orderly one. One man was scouring the edge of the plateau, looking for any sign that the three men and two kids had climbed over the edge. The rest of the men were moving clockwise around the plateau, searching everything in their path.

Roland and Axel were watching carefully. They knew it was a matter of time before the search would center on the temple, and then there would be men all over the place. They had hoped they could hold out for nightfall, but that hope was fading rapidly.

C.J. leaned against the wall. He didn't know what Sadie meant. The things his dad taught him didn't help him figure out how to get away from somebody trying to capture or kill you.

He dug his foot into the debris and watched the sand roll off his shoe. He looked over to where his father was lying, and then he noticed it.

His tracks led from where he had been sitting near his father to where he was leaning against the wall. Next to one of his tracks was another larger footprint in the sand. Roland and Axel hadn't been back that far. Someone else had been there.

He stood up and glanced around. There was another track closer to the wall. There was something else that was odd. The sand in front of one section of the wall lay smoothed out on one side and piled up on the other.

He looked closer at the wall. What had Scotty said? The Inca could make a wall that was earthquake resistant. What else? Then he remembered.

If they placed a stone just right, it could pivot open like a door. He pushed on one side of the wall, but nothing happened. He tried the other side where the sand lay piled up. Again, nothing happened. He tried pushing harder, and it pushed in a little.

Unfortunately, the movement also created a loud grinding noise.

Roland and Axel spun around and saw C.J. standing by the wall.

"What are you doing?" Roland asked. He didn't wait for an answer though as both he and Axel turned back toward the men out on the plateau.

Freitag had heard the noise and was sending his men up toward the temple.

"People are coming," Roland called to the others. "We need to get hidden again."

Roland and Axel covered Angus and the two kids with debris again. Then the two of them brushed the sand, hiding the tracks they had made. Finally, Axel covered Roland.

Axel heard the men coming up the steps as he brushed his tracks and ducked behind the statue. He glanced at the mounds and froze.

Angus's hand stuck out of the sand. He heard the searchers nearing the top of the steps. There was no time to cover his hand.

He pulled the knife that he'd picked up in the infirmary and held it ready to throw.

When the searchers reached the top of the steps, they peered over the fallen columns into the secluded area. Everything looked as it did the first time they looked. They moved along the pillar, but they saw nothing suspicious.

They were about to give up again when Hayes stopped the other man.

"What is that?" he asked, pointing toward the pile where Axel had tried to hide Angus.

"What?" Palmer asked.

"There, by that pile of rocks." The men squinted at it, but it was too far for them to make it out.

"Give me a hand," Hayes said. Palmer stooped to help him get up and over the broken column.

Axel saw Hayes climb over the column. He held the knife ready. He would wait for the man to get close enough where he could kill him and take his weapon.

The man sat on the column, ready to slide down on the other side. He tried to make out what was sticking out of the pile of rocks. He slid off the column and landed on the soft sand next to it.

Hayes drew his pistol and held it ready. He slowly stepped forward and narrowed his eyes at the object on the ground.

"Can you see it?" Palmer called.

"Not yet," Hayes said, taking another step.

Axel was flat on his stomach. His hands were palm down on the sand on either side of him, ready to spring to his feet. He listened for the sounds of the man's progress.

Hayes stopped and aimed his pistol. He carefully squeezed the trigger.

The sound of the shot echoed off the rock walls. Axel shut his eyes. The man had shot at Angus. He was still too far away for Axel to attack. At that distance, the man would shoot Axel, too. He just hoped that Angus was still alive and that he could get to him in time.

"Just a rat," Hayes said and walked back to the column. He ran the last few steps and jumped up onto it. He was about to slide off the other side when they all heard a far different noise.

There was an explosion out on the plateau.

"What was that?" he asked.

There was a second explosion.

He quickly slid back down to the steps and then all the men were running back toward camp.

Axel looked over the top of the statue and saw that the men were gone. He ran to Angus and quickly dug him out. Roland and the two kids shook off the debris piles and hurried over to help Axel. When they uncovered Angus, they were relieved to find that the man was unhurt.

Glancing around, Roland found the rat that the man had shot. "Our only casualty," he said.

Roland and Axel went to see about the source of the explosions.

Where one tent once stood, there was a blackened hole. Another tent was burning. The men had abandoned their search and were dumping buckets of sand over the flames. Freitag and Eberhardt were yelling, but neither Axel nor Roland could hear what they were saying.

Axel pointed at some rocks above the pyramid. Roland looked and could see Axel's son, Frederick, and Walter MacGregor preparing more explosives.

Before they could see what Frederick and Walter had in mind for their next target, they heard the grinding sound again. When they looked behind them, they saw a smiling C.J. pointing to an opening in the wall next to him.

They ran to the door and found that it led down to a hidden room. Quickly, they got Angus and the two kids into it. Then they cleaned up their tracks.

"Stay with them," Axel told Roland. "I'm going to help Frederick and Walter."

Roland nodded and climbed down into the room. They pivoted the door closed again, leaving the four of them in the dark.

Chapter 11

They didn't think about the need for light until Axel closed the door and left them in total darkness. Roland grabbed a matchbox out of his pocket and lit a match.

In the dim light of the match, they scrambled around, looking for something that could provide them with light. After a few seconds, Roland waved the match, and the light was gone again. C.J. and Sadie heard another strike of a match. The dim light returned, and the scramble continued.

This time, C.J. found a kerosene lantern and soon the room was lit up with its yellowish glow.

It wasn't a large room, but members of the other expedition made it even smaller when they stacked several crates against one wall. Fortunately, Roland and the kids had enough room to make themselves comfortable until Axel and the others came back for them.

Roland checked the door. It was closed all the way, which would make it difficult to spot from outside unless you already knew where it was. And the crates in the room showed that someone from the camp knew it was there.

"I hope Axel and Walter can keep them busy so that nobody comes to check on this room," Roland said, listening at the door.

C.J. and Sadie looked at each other. The worry showed in their faces.

Satisfied that no one was outside the door at the moment, Roland checked out the rest of the room.

Against one wall near the door, there was a folding table with a telegraph machine on it. Piled next to the machine were several notebooks. Roland looked through some of them.

"They're all in German," he said. "Probably code books used for sending messages."

"What's that?" C.J. asked. A wire ran from the machine up through the rocks in the ceiling.

"They must have connected it to an antenna hidden somewhere in the temple ruins above us," Roland told him.

"This must be what they used to send the message we heard," Sadie said.

Roland agreed with Sadie. He moved a few more notebooks and discovered a thin, leather briefcase. He cleared the notebooks off and tried to open it. "It's locked," he said.

"How can we open it?" C.J. asked. "Is there a key?"

"No need," Roland said with a grin. He pulled out the knife that Axel had given him and quickly pried open the case. Inside were several official-looking documents.

Roland glanced at them. "They're all in German," he said.

"Of course," Sadie said.

"Some of them have what appear to be official government seals," Roland said. "This operation must be very important to somebody." He threw the papers back into the case and shut it.

Roland looked around the room and then went over to the stack of crates. "I wonder what they're storing down here," he said.

"Extra supplies?" C.J. asked.

"Let's find out," Roland said and pried the lid up on one crate with the knife. He put the knife away and pulled the lid the rest of the way off.

Inside were rocks just like the one C.J. had picked up by the pyramid.

C.J. picked one of them out of the crate. "What do you think they are?" he asked. "Gold? Diamonds?"

"I doubt they're diamonds," Roland said. "Probably gold, like Jackson said." He pried the lids off several other crates. They all held rocks like the others.

"Whatever they are," Sadie said, "they want a lot of them."

Roland looked around the room. "I guess the telegraph is the only thing that might be of use to us," he said. He went back over to the table and sat down at the machine.

After studying the control panel, he flicked a couple of switches and waited. A few moments later, he announced, "It seems to work."

"Let's send for help," C.J. said.

"My thoughts exactly," Roland said. He grabbed a sheet of paper and began writing a message. When he was done, he looked up at C.J. "Do you think you can send this?"

C.J. took the paper and read it. "What does 'By the pricking of my thumbs' mean at the end?" he asked.

"It's a code. Can you send it?" Roland asked again.

"Sure," he said.

"Do it then," Roland told him.

C.J. sat down at the device and tapped out dots and dashes as he translated the message into Morse code to send to the ship.

Roland and Sadie watched him as he moved his finger across the page and then onto the next line, converting each letter into the appropriate signals.

When he reached the end of the message, C.J. asked, "Should I repeat it?"

"That would be a good idea," Roland told him.

C.J. repeated the message again. When he finished, he looked up at Roland. "Now what?"

"Now we wait," Roland said, "and hope that someone on the ship was listening."

C.J. sat back in the chair while Sadie sat down on the floor and leaned back against a crate.

Roland kneeled down next to Angus and checked his pulse and breathing.

"Is he OK?" C.J. asked.

"He should be fine," Roland told him. "I'd be happy if we could get him to a doctor soon."

Roland stood up and went to a crate. He sat on top of it and leaned back on the crates behind it. He closed his eyes and rested.

C.J. went over and sat next to his father and leaned against the rock wall. He wished his father would wake up.

Sadie sat down by C.J. He glanced over at her and found that she was looking at him oddly. He looked down at the dusty floor next to him and drew a quick diagram of the plateau with the temple, pyramid, and tents. He looked back at Sadie, and she was still staring at him.

"What?" C.J. asked.

"How did we get here?" she asked.

"On the ship?" C.J. asked.

"No, I mean, how did we get in here?" she repeated.

"Bad luck," he said and looked back at the diagram in the dust. He ran his hand over it and erased it.

"It wasn't luck," she told him.

"What was it then?"

"You figured out the secret."

"The secret?" he asked.

"You didn't need your dad to figure out how to get out of trouble," Sadie told him. "You already had the information you needed to get out of trouble."

"We were lucky this room was here," C.J. said.

"Maybe, but it wasn't luck that you found the hidden door," she said. "You found it because they taught you to be observant, and you figured it out."

"OK, maybe I figured out one thing," C.J. admitted.

"Was it luck that you knew Morse code?" she asked. "Or were we able to call for help because of something you learned to do?"

"Two things," C.J. said. He looked away. He knew she was right. They weren't lucky. He looked back. She was still looking at him.

"Stop that," he told her.

Suddenly, the telegraph erupted with dots and dashes. C.J. quickly grabbed a sheet of paper and scribbled furiously.

Roland and Sadie waited for the message to finish. It did, and then it repeated.

Once C.J. realized that he had the full message, he gave the paper to Roland. "Why did they end with 'something wicked this way comes'?" he asked.

"It's the answer to my code. I gave the first part of the code to identify me," he told them, "and they gave the response to identify them."

When he finished reading the message, he looked at the two kids. "They'll try to get us some help."

"How long will it be?" Sadie asked.

"I don't know," Roland told her. "Several hours."

Just then, they heard a sound at the door. Roland turned toward it. The knife was in his hand.

"Is it Eberhardt?" C.J. whispered.

"I don't know," Roland said.

They heard the sound again. It sounded like someone scratching at the door. C.J. rushed over to it and listened. He could hear a muffled whine.

Roland told him to get away from the door. But before he could do anything to stop him, C.J. pushed on the door to pivot it open a little. A black dog bounded into the room.

C.J. pivoted the door shut again as the dog ran past everyone and sat down next to Angus.

"What were you thinking?" Roland asked. "It could have been a trap."

"No," C.J. said. "It wouldn't have come here if there had been anyone else out there." He slowly approached the dog.

"Stay back," Roland said.

"It's OK," C.J. told him. He eased closer to the dog, almost getting close enough to touch it.

The dog looked down at the unconscious man and curled up beside him.

A few moments later, Angus moved, and with a groan, opened his eyes.

C.J. forgot all about the dog and went to his father. "Dad, you're all right?"

The dog quickly got up and moved away from Angus as Roland and Sadie rushed over to him. Angus told them he was weak, but he wanted to sit up. They helped him into a sitting position and leaned him against the wall.

He glanced around the room in confusion. "What's been happening?"

The three of them took turns filling him in on the events of the last several hours. They told him about how the creature attacked him and that the wraith was actually the ghost of an Inca boy. They told him about being held prisoner and their escape and how they ended up in the hidden room.

"I guess our plan didn't work out as well as we would've liked," he joked.

"We have two things going for us," Roland told him. "Walter and Axel are still out there, keeping them busy."

"You hope," Angus interrupted.

"Yes," Roland said. "I hope. And we got a message from the ship. They're going to send help."

Angus was going to say something again, but Roland headed him off.

"Yes," Roland said again. "I hope."

Angus looked at his son. "I'm proud of you, C.J. If it weren't for you, I wouldn't be alive." He pulled his son to him and gave him a hug.

"And because of you, we could escape Eberhardt and find refuge in this place."

"I was just prepared," C.J. told him. "Sadie said that anything we learn might help us when we're in trouble," C.J. told him.

Angus smiled at Sadie. "She sounds like a wise young lady," he said.

C.J. looked at Sadie, who smiled proudly.

Angus stretched and complained about his back, so Roland and C.J. helped him into the chair so that he could be more comfortable.

"How long is it before help can arrive?" Angus asked Roland.

"Still several hours, I'd guess," Roland said. "They will have to persuade the authorities in Lima to come out here."

"I hope it won't be too late," Angus said.

Almost in answer, the door pivoted open.

Chapter 12

As the door swung open, Roland quickly drew his knife to lunge at the first person who came through. When he realized it was Axel, he checked his swing. Axel and Frederick came through the door and pushed the door almost closed again.

"I'm glad to see you," Roland said.

"It didn't seem like it," Axel joked.

When Axel saw Angus sitting in the chair, he was relieved. "I thought we might have lost you this time," Axel told him.

"I've got at least one more life left," Angus said.

"Where's Walter?" Roland asked.

"He's outside keeping an eye out," Axel said.

"What's the situation?" Roland asked.

"We bombarded the camp until everyone had headed for cover," Axel told them. "If someone showed their face, we'd hit them again."

"Where are they now?" Angus asked.

"We have seen no one for almost an hour," Frederick said. "They're still hiding in their tents."

"What about you, Angus?" Axel asked. "How are you doing?"

"I'm weak, but I'm doing OK," he told them.

"We sent a message to the Falcon," Roland said, jerking his thumb at the telegraph.

"When do you expect help to arrive?" Axel asked.

"Not for a while," Roland told him.

Axel's hand went to his pistol. "What's that?"

Everyone turned to see what he was looking at. The dark shape of the dog padded out from the shadows of the crates.

"It's a dog," C.J. said. "He lives somewhere around here. Sadie and I saw him outside the other night."

Axel relaxed. "What's it doing in here?"

"C.J. heard scratching at the door," Roland said. "He let him in."

"How did you know it wasn't a trap?" Axel asked.

"That's what I asked," Roland answered for him. "He didn't."

"There's something special about him," C.J. said. "After he sat down beside my dad, my dad woke up."

"It's just a coincidence," Roland said.

C.J. shook his head.

"We need to decide what we're going to do," Axel said, ignoring C.J.

"You know the situation better than us," Angus said. "What do you think we should do?"

"We should head down the mountain as soon as possible," Axel told them.

"Will they try to stop us?" Roland asked.

"I don't think so. They're hiding in their tents," Axel told him. "They'll just be glad we're gone."

"What do you think, Angus?" Roland asked.

"I'll try to keep up," Angus said. "If I can't, you'll need to get the kids to safety first."

"We won't leave you behind," Roland said.

Axel opened the door again and looked out. Everyone else prepared to move out of the room.

Outside, Walter leaned on a column and watched the bombed out camp. He signaled everything was all clear.

They crossed the secluded area of the temple ruins and waited at the column. After they had checked again that there was no sign of anyone around the camp, they climbed over the column and hurried down the steps.

They just reached the bottom of the steps and were about to head for the edge of the bluff, when the sound of gunfire rang out, and two bullets ricocheted among the rocks.

They scattered and found rocks to hide behind. Roland peered around the side of a wall to see where the shots came from.

Two men were hiding just below the edge of the bluff, right where they were headed.

"It's Granville and Hayes," Axel called out.

"How did they get there?" Angus asked.

"They sneaked out of the tents somehow," Walter told him. "I bet they crawled down along the gully under the rope bridge."

"Anybody hurt?" Roland called out.

One by one, they called out their status. Nobody was hurt.

Axel whispered to him. "I'll try to keep them busy here. You move around the other side of the temple. Go down the hill that way and get into the trees."

Roland nodded. He passed the message on to the rest. As soon as everyone was ready, Axel turned toward the two men at the edge of the plateau.

When Axel shot twice at Granville and Hayes, Roland gathered the others and they headed out onto the plateau, keeping the temple ruins between them and the two men at the edge of the bluff.

As they hurried across the plateau, C.J. whispered to Sadie. "We're going back down to where we came up." He pointed ahead to the spot they had hidden that morning. Sadie nodded.

They were about halfway there when they heard Axel running after them.

"They're coming!" he yelled.

They raced to the edge. Angus, breathing hard, found it difficult to keep up. Walter gave his pistol to Roland and slowed to help Angus. Angus threw his arm over Walter's shoulder, and Walter helped support him as they ran.

As they neared the edge, Freitag and Jensen popped up from below the edge and fired at them. They veered off toward the pyramid and ran to find shelter among the rocks off to the side. Bullets kicked up sand and dust wherever they hit the ground.

Axel fired at the two men as Roland rushed the kids toward the rocks and helped them up and behind them. He then turned back to Walter and Angus.

Angus looked as if he were about to collapse. Roland ran back to help Walter steady him while Axel provided cover fire.

They made it to the rocks and immediately ducked down behind the largest ones. The dog followed.

"Thanks for your help, Walter," Angus said between breaths when he was sitting behind a rock and leaning against it.

"What now?" Axel asked.

Roland glanced around. "We can't climb the mountain," he said. "If we stay here too long, we might end up being trapped."

Roland looked out at the terraces that ran down the mountain to the ocean below. "If we can make it there," he said, pointing beyond the tents. "We can hide in the tall grass and make our way down."

"Sounds good to me," Walter said.

Before they could move, Eberhardt and Palmer came out of the tent and fired at them.

"Now what?" Roland asked.

"We have two more bombs," Walter told him. "If we throw one at Freitag and the other at Eberhardt, it should give us a few moments to move."

"To where?" Roland asked.

"The pyramid," Axel said.

"No," Roland said.

"We won't last long out here," Axel said.

"I agree," Angus said.

Roland looked back at the men converging on them across the plateau. "I guess we don't have any better choices," he said.

When Freitag saw the bomb drop in front of him, he only had seconds to turn and run before it exploded and knocked him several feet through the air.

Though the sound of the explosion muffled his hearing and a constant ringing filled his ears, he could hear another explosion farther away. He got to his feet and looked across the plateau.

Eberhardt and the other man were sprawled in the dirt, recovering from the bomb that had detonated near them.

He glanced toward where Angus and his men had taken refuge, but he couldn't see them. Out of the corner of his eye, he saw movement and when he turned toward the pyramid, he just caught sight of the last of them disappearing through the entrance.

He smiled. "We have them trapped!" he yelled. It was even hard to hear himself with his hearing messed up.

Once the four men, the three kids and the dog were all inside the pyramid, they realized they didn't have any lanterns to protect them from the dark. Axel and Roland each grabbed a torch off the wall and hoped that they would last long enough to get back out again.

Roland told them to continue down the corridor into the pyramid and away from the entrance. "We need to get out of line of sight," he told them. "We don't want them to shoot us through the doorway."

As they disappeared around a corner, they heard the first shots behind them.

When they reached the steps down, Roland pointed further down the corridor on the same level. "Let's try down this way," he said and started walking in that direction.

The dog, however, padded down the first couple of steps and then looked back at the group. When they didn't immediately follow him, he whined.

C.J. stopped and called to the dog. The dog looked down the steps and back at C.J.

"He wants us to go down the steps," C.J. said.

"I think we should stay on this level," Roland said.

"I think he's trying to help us," C.J. protested.

Roland looked at Angus for help with his son.

Angus looked at C.J. and after a moment, surprised everyone by saying, "C.J.'s judgment has gone a long way to getting us out of one predicament after another today. I think we should trust in him again."

Despite another protest by Roland, they followed the dog down the steps to the door of the hall of sarcophagi. They stopped at the door and watched the dog go in.

"As good a place as any for a last stand," Axel said.

They went in and used the torches to light the torches in wall sconces around the room. They cast a dim light throughout.

"Axel, Walter, and I have weapons," Roland said. "The rest of you find a place to hide."

They each found a spot to shield them from sight and waited. The dog sat down by C.J., closed his eyes and cocked his head to one side. It was almost as if he were listening for something.

The wait wasn't long. They heard Freitag, Eberhardt, and the other men come down the steps and pause outside the door.

"This is the end, gentlemen," Freitag called in to them. "You've troubled us for the last time."

Shots rang out. In the enclosed room, they seemed extremely loud. All the kids covered their ears.

Each time they fired, one man slipped into the room and took a position so that soon they had much of the room covered. Finally, Freitag himself moved into the room and watched down one of the center paths between the sarcophagi.

"On my signal," he told his men, "open fire."

Eberhardt was about to move into the room when suddenly everything changed.

The dog began barking as a dark form flew through the doorway into the room, causing Eberhardt to lose his balance and fall backward into the outer room.

The shadow flew around the ceiling of the room, weaving in and around the four pillars that held the ceiling up. Each time it flew near where C.J. and the dog had hidden, the dog would bark at it.

Several shots rang out as Freitag's men tried to shoot at the shadow uselessly. Freitag shouted at them to stop shooting. He called to Eberhardt, but there was no answer from the man.

The wraith suddenly stopped. It hovered in the center of the room for a few moments. Then it began its attack, and the screaming started.

Chapter 13

They watched in horror as the wraith attacked one man after another. The chilling screams of the victims echoed throughout the room.

It chased Palmer, who, once he realized he would not escape, turned at the wraith and desperately emptied his clip into the shadowy form. The wraith enveloped him, and within seconds, it reduced Palmer to a pile of dusty clothes and bones.

Jensen sliced at it with a large Bowie knife, but both the knife and his arm went right through the misty body of the wraith. The knife came out unharmed while the flesh of his arm dried up and broke away. The man's screams ended moments later.

As the wraith made its way through the room, C.J. tried to see where Freitag and Eberhardt were. There was no sign of them.

Then he realized when Freitag's men scattered about the room, it made it easy for the wraith to pick them off one by one. "Everyone, get together in a group," he yelled.

Everyone quickly joined C.J. at the end of the room and stood as one with Roland, Angus, and C.J. in front. The black dog sat at C.J.'s feet.

"Throw away your guns and knives," C.J. told them. "We don't want to look threatening. They won't do us any good, anyway."

They all threw away their weapons to the side.

As the wraith swept toward Hayes, the man cut across the room and ran straight at Granville. He grabbed the man and turned toward the wraith. The wraith did not stop. Hayes pushed Granville into the wraith and tried to run again.

Granville, however, grabbed onto Hayes to escape the wraith. It didn't work. The wraith wrapped around him. As the life was being drained from the man, his arm kept its vice-like grip on Hayes.

The arm disappeared into the wraith, pulling Hayes with it. Hayes clawed at Granville's fingers, but it was too late. The wraith slowly drew the man into it. His screaming began as his arm disappeared into the shadowy form and ended just after it drew his head in.

As Hayes' screams died off, they saw Freitag jump up from behind a sarcophagus and dash out the door.

C.J. pointed toward the man disappearing up the steps. "Freitag's getting away," C.J. told them.

"If we ever get out of here, he won't," Angus said. "We'll be witnesses to his crimes, and he won't find a place in the world where he can hide."

With no others in the room to attack, the wraith came at the group and stopped in front of them. They all shrank back against the wall, as far away from the wraith as they could get.

C.J. tried to remind the wraith that they had met before. He tapped his chest and then that of his father next to him.

The wraith didn't immediately attack. It hovered and watched them.

It became enraged. It expanded in size until it was almost twice its normal size and rushed toward them.

Before the wraith could reach them, the black dog jumped at it and barked furiously.

The wraith instantly fell back and shrank until it was its original size, if not a little smaller.

The dog stopped his barking and sat down in front of the group. It watched the dark shape.

The shape changed, and C.J. thought it might turn into the Inca boy again.

Before it could fully change, the dog barked at it again. Immediately, it went back to its shadowy form and a moment later, flew out of the room.

No one moved for more than a minute. They all expected the wraith to come swooping back into the room. They let out a collective sigh of relief as they rushed to grab their weapons. They left the dead men behind as they quickly left the room.

They carefully made their way up the steps. Freitag, Eberhardt, or the wraith could have been anywhere, and they didn't want to stumble into any of them. They got to the top of the steps and picked up the pace as they neared the pyramid entrance.

After they rushed out onto the plateau and into the light of the setting sun, they halted.

Freitag was standing in the middle of the plateau, his hands over his head. Several members of the Peruvian Army surrounded him with their weapons trained on him. The cavalry unit spread out, facing them with their weapons raised. A couple dozen horses stood in a group by the tents.

The leader of the troop, a tall lieutenant with a sword at his side, stepped forward and, in English with a heavy accent, said, "Drop your weapons and place your hands on your heads, gentlemen."

They complied with his orders.

As one soldier gathered up their weapons, another soldier came from the camp and said something to the lieutenant. He turned to them.

"Is there anyone else that we should know about?" he asked.

Freitag shook his head.

"Four of his men," Angus said, pointing to Freitag, "are in the pyramid. But they're dead. One of his men is missing."

The lieutenant raised an eyebrow. "You killed them?" he asked Angus.

"No," Angus said.

"Who did?" the lieutenant asked.

"You wouldn't believe me."

"Try me."

"A wraith."

"A wraith?" the lieutenant asked. Several of his men laughed.

"Yes," Angus said. "It is the ghost of a young Inca boy. There is another man, an old man, in the infirmary. He was also a victim of the wraith."

"We know about him," the lieutenant said. "Unfortunately, he was already dead when we arrived."

"Wait a minute," a familiar voice said from behind the line of men. "Wait just a minute." Jackson Hall broke through the line and approached the lieutenant. Teresa and Laura Hall, Edna MacGregor, and her son, Scotty, followed him.

"They are the ones that needed rescuing," Jackson said, pointing at Angus and the others. Then he pointed at Freitag. "He's the one that was holding them against their will," he told the officer.

"It looks like we got here just in time," the lieutenant joked. "They had him outnumbered seven to one."

"There is no need to be pointing weapons at them," Jackson told him.

The lieutenant signaled his men to stand down. "You may put your hands down," he told them. "But you will be required to stay here until we have this sorted out."

"We have someone who needs medical attention," Roland said, nodding to Angus.

"I will have a medic check him out," the lieutenant said. "Beyond that, he will have to wait until we return to Lima."

He nodded to one of his men, who moved forward to check Angus's condition.

"You didn't capture anyone else?" Roland asked.

"No," the lieutenant said, "just this man and then the seven of you."

"We need to watch the entrance of the pyramid," Roland told him. "Living or dead, Eberhardt must still be inside."

The lieutenant arranged for a pair of guards at the entrance. Freitag was bound, and all the adults went with the lieutenant and his men to tell them what had been going on for the past couple of days.

The five young explorers gathered in their own group to catch up on the news.

C.J. and Sadie related their adventures from when they left the truck early that morning until they ended up in the hidden room.

Frederick joined in at that point telling them how he, his dad and Walter MacGregor kept the camp in chaos, throwing bombs and destroying tents.

All three of them took turns telling about their ill-fated escape attempt and the wraith attack in the pyramid. C.J. finished up telling Laura and Scotty how the black dog saved them from the wraith.

Laura was looking at the dog thoughtfully.

"What?" C.J. asked her.

"When I went back to the ship," she said, "I read everything I could find on the Inca civilization again."

"Again?" C.J. asked.

"Again," Scotty said with a sigh.

Laura ignored their comments. "I tried to find out about their religious beliefs and the afterlife."

"What does all that have to do with the dog?" C.J. asked her.

"Everything," Laura said. "After death, they would wrap the body with cotton to form a mummy. Sometimes they would wrap together several members of the same family."

"Creepy," Scotty said.

"Up here," she said, "the dry, windy mountain air would dry the bodies into natural mummies."

"And the dog?" C.J. prompted her.

"They placed the mummies into tombs," Laura said, "and surrounded them with things that they thought the departed would need in the afterlife."

"They did that in the pyramid here," Sadie said.

"But for the departed to find their way through to where their ancestors dwell, they would need to enlist the aid of a mystical black dog that some call a Lazaro."

"Finally," C.J. said. "And you think this dog could be a Lazaro?"

"I'm not saying that," Laura said. "I'm just saying he's a black dog and a black dog is important to the Inca afterlife."

"You think he's here for the wraith?" Sadie asked.

"Why didn't he go with him then?" C.J. asked.

"Maybe he's been a wraith for so long, he doesn't remember," Sadie said.

They all fell silent and looked at the dog. The thought that this dog could have something to do with the Inca afterlife was exciting to them.

"If we can get the boy to go with the dog," Sadie said, "then he can rest in peace, and we can rid the pyramid of the wraith."

"But how?" Scotty asked.

"I've got it," C.J. suddenly blurted out.

"What?" Sadie asked.

"We're going back inside the pyramid," C.J. told them, "tonight."

Chapter 14

"Why are we going back into the pyramid?" Frederick asked.

"What's your plan?" Sadie interrupted.

"We're going to have a funeral for the Inca boy," C.J. told them. "If we can lay him to rest, maybe the dog can lead him on."

"Maybe," Sadie said.

"What if this is just a regular dog and not a — What did you call it?" Scotty asked.

"A Lazaro," Laura told him.

"Yes," Scotty said. "What if it isn't a Lazaro?"

"I don't know," C.J. said. They were all silent for a while.

"What do we need?" Sadie asked.

C.J. gave them a list of the things they would need. Frederick, Laura, and Scotty went to get their assigned objects. Sadie stayed with C.J.

"What about our parents?" Sadie asked.

"I'll take care of them," C.J. told her.

One-by-one, the young explorers gathered the things they would need.

Laura searched through the main tent. She found cloth that the original expedition used to pack artifacts for shipment back to the United States. She grabbed the cloth and returned to the meeting place.

Frederick and Scotty also scoured through the main tent. They tried to find several items each that looked as if it could have belonged to a young Inca boy. After they had each discovered three or four items, they also returned.

C.J. and Sadie located the most important item for the funeral. They left the main tent carrying a large bundle wrapped in cloth between them.

Angus was talking with Roland when he saw the kids gathering together with their bundles. He excused himself and went to where they were standing.

"What are you up to?" Angus asked.

C.J. and Laura told him about what she had learned about the Inca afterlife and the significance of the black dog.

"We want to have a funeral for the boy," C.J. said, finishing up the story. "Maybe he'll leave with the dog and we won't have to worry about the wraith leaving the pyramid and getting loose in the world."

Angus looked thoughtfully at the five of them. Finally, he said, "It's worth a try." He looked back at the lieutenant talking with some of his men and gesturing toward the pyramid. "The lieutenant may have plans of his own for the pyramid."

Angus led the young explorers over to where the lieutenant was talking to his men.

"Ah, Mr. Kask, you are just the person who can help us," the lieutenant told him.

"If I can," Angus said.

"I am sending a squad into the pyramid to search for this Dr. Eberhardt. We would like you to tell us precisely where you saw him last."

"I can do better than that," Angus said. "I can show you."

"You would go back into the pyramid?"

Angus gestured at the kids and the things that they were carrying. "We were just talking about returning some of these artifacts to their place in the pyramid," he told him. "And that is right where we saw him last."

The lieutenant narrowed his eyes at Angus. C.J. and the other young explorers weren't sure that he was going to believe them, but then he nodded. "Very well," he said.

Angus added Roland and Axel to the group to help protect the kids and then they all gathered at the entrance to the pyramid when the lieutenant and his men were ready.

"I would recommend that you leave your weapons outside the pyramid," Angus told them. "The wraith dislikes weapons and seems to attack anyone who has one, including those." Angus pointed at the lieutenant's sword hanging at his belt.

"What if Dr. Eberhardt has a weapon?"

"If he does," Angus said, "then we probably don't have to worry about finding him alive."

Reluctantly, the lieutenant followed his advice. He left several armed guards outside the pyramid to make sure that Dr. Eberhardt didn't escape.

The group made their way down into the pyramid with the dog. They had an abundance of lanterns and several torches, by a request from C.J. They shined the lanterns into every nook and cranny along the way, checking for both the wraith and Dr. Eberhardt.

When they made it to the sarcophagi room, they found the original torches were still burning but had almost burned out.

When they entered the room, they spread out to check for Dr. Eberhardt. They found the remains of Freitag's four men as they came across the three piles of bones one after another.

"I'm starting to believe your story," the Lieutenant told Angus. He ordered his men to gather up the bodies so that they can transport them up to the surface.

They gathered up Palmer and Jensen and wrapped their bones in the remnants of their clothes. Granville and Hayes presented a problem. Since their bones mixed, the soldiers wrapped them together in a single bundle to be sorted out later.

As they passed the failing torches, they replaced them with the new ones and extinguished the remains of the old ones. When they finished, they covered the lanterns. The torches lit the room bright enough to see, but not so bright as to scare the wraith away.

C.J. and the young explorers carefully moved a mummy and its possessions from the center stone block to an empty one near the side. C.J. and Sadie solemnly placed their large bundle in the newly emptied center block.

C.J. unwrapped it a little to show the face.

"It's the body of the Inca boy," C.J. said. "Freitag said they found it just inside the pyramid entrance."

Laura looked away. She didn't want to think about how the boy had died alone in the dark. Sadie and Scotty gazed at the face of the unknown boy.

"This boy died in here without a funeral," C.J. told them. "If he is the wraith, this might help him pass over to the other side."

They wrapped the cloth back around him and then wrapped him further with the cloth that Laura brought. Once it was done, Frederick and Scotty placed the artifacts around the body.

Several of the military men crossed themselves.

Scotty nudged Sadie. "What is that about?"

"Many of the people in Peru are Catholics," Sadie whispered back. "Some use the sign of the cross to call on God's blessing or as a protection against evil."

Scotty nodded and then pointed to a nearby mummy that was far larger than the rest. "That must be one of those that have more than one mummy wrapped together," he said.

The rest of the group just stared at it. To them, it was a strange thing to do. "I will stay by the mummy with the dog," C.J. told them. "The rest of you should probably stand back near the wall."

"I will stay with you," Angus told C.J.

C.J. nodded. "You have a connection with the dog."

"I want to stay too," Sadie said.

"I want you to be safe," C.J. told her. "I don't want you where you might get hurt accidentally or—"

"Or what?" she asked.

"In case I'm wrong about the dog," C.J. said.

Sadie frowned at him. "I don't need you to protect me, C.J. Kask," she said. "I can protect myself, thank you very much." She stood with her arms folded across her chest and looked at him with a look that said, "Don't you dare contradict me."

C.J. was quiet for a moment and then said, "You're right, Sadie. I'm sorry."

Her glare softened, and she unfolded her arms. "You're forgiven." She kneeled down beside the dog and gingerly pet it.

The lieutenant ordered his men to stand with the others. "I will stay with you also," he told C.J.

"Thank you," C.J. said. "But I think your uniform might be a trigger for the wraith, like the weapons."

The lieutenant glanced down at his uniform and considered what the boy had said. Finally, he nodded and went to join the others.

The others stood and watched. The members of Angus's group worried about the appearance of the wraith. The members of the Peruvian Army weren't sure what they were going to see.

"How do you know it will appear?" the lieutenant asked Laura.

"I don't," Laura confessed. "I think C.J. is only guessing, but his instincts are good. I trust him."

The lieutenant looked at Laura and then at the young boy standing in the middle of the room. "You put a lot of trust in him," the lieutenant said. "I hope, for the sake of all of us, he's right."

C.J. also hoped that he'd be right again. "Do you think it will work?" he asked his father.

"Your theory about the wraith makes sense," Angus told him. "The rest of us didn't know what to do."

"But will it work?" C.J. asked.

"You just have to come up with a plan to solve the problem," Angus said, "and carry it through to the end." He clapped his son on the shoulder. "That's the only way to know for sure."

C.J. smiled at his father.

Angus continued, "I'm proud of you for speaking up and putting yourself out there." He put an arm around his son and gave him a little hug.

Then the dog moved. It stood up and acted as if it were listening. All conversations in the room died down as everyone listened to see if they could hear what the dog had heard.

The dog took a step forward and stopped again. He whined a bit and then was silent. C.J. could see that he was listening again.

Everyone stared at the door, waiting for the wraith.

The dog barked once again and then broke into a run. He quickly ran out of the room and up the stairs.

C.J. was in shock. The key part of his plan just ran out the door. What were they going to do now?

Amid his confusion, he heard an odd sound nearby. He couldn't tell where it came from. He looked around the room.

"Did you hear that, Dad?" he asked.

"Hear what?" his father asked.

Then everyone could hear a sound approaching. It was the sound of a distant wind coming nearer from outside the room.

"Is that the wraith?" the lieutenant asked Laura.

"I think so," she told him.

The military men automatically reached for their weapons before remembering that they didn't have any. They were trained for combat, but this was well beyond anyone's training.

Although scared, everyone in the room had the same question in their minds. What were they going to do without the dog?

Then, with a screech, the wraith entered the room.

Chapter 15

The wraith zoomed through the room until it came to a stop by the center stone in front of C.J., Sadie, and Angus. Angus put his hand on C.J.'s shoulder.

After several tense moments, the wraith moved again. It flew up and around the room, snaking between the columns that held the ceiling up. It came to a stop in front of the group at the end of the room.

The lieutenant barked an order, and his men formed a wall in front of the civilians. Despite their fear of the creature, they stood their ground.

The wraith grew in size again and moved toward the line of men.

"No," C.J. shouted.

The wraith shrank away and flew around the room wildly. After several passes extremely close to both groups, it flew to the center of the room and stopped in front of C.J.

"We are friends," C.J. said, trying to sound calm despite his fear of the wraith. He tapped his chest to remind the wraith of his connection to his father. But he pointed to the wraith instead.

The wraith shrank back to its normal size and the frenzied movements it had been making calmed until it just floated in front of C.J.

C.J. took a step forward toward the mummy on the center block. The step also took him closer to the wraith. He kept his eyes on the wraith in case it made any move toward him.

He reached over the mummy and pulled the wrappings back that covered its face. He pointed to the face and then pointed to the wraith.

The wraith shrank back, away from the block.

C.J. tapped his chest and then tapped the chest of the mummy. He hoped the wraith would understand. He was trying to tell the wraith that he was a friend and he was trying to help him.

C.J. then backed away from the mummy toward his father. The wraith floated forward and glided slowly around the stone as if it were looking at everything on it.

Tendrils of shadow reached out from the wraith and passed over the things they had placed around the mummy. It paused over the two pyramidal dice and then continued around. When the wraith reached the exposed face, it stopped as if it were staring down at it.

Everyone in the room stood silent and unmoving. Their eyes were all on the wraith.

As everyone watched, the wraith shrank down, and the darkness faded until it was again just the image of a young Inca boy.

The boy continued to gaze down at his mummified face lying on the stone. He looked up at C.J. and smiled. He tapped his chest and pointed at C.J.

C.J. smiled at him. He hoped the boy could rest at peace, knowing his body was ready for his afterlife.

C.J. glanced toward the door of the room. If only the dog were here, he thought.

Just then, the double mummy lying beside C.J. rolled over, fell to the floor and came to rest at C.J.'s feet. Everyone jumped at the sudden movement.

Dr. Eberhardt startled them again when he leapt up from the space where the mummy had been lying. He pulled a large knife from a sheath and held it out toward C.J.

The image of the Inca boy dissolved immediately into the inky blackness of the shadowy wraith. It stretched upward and towered over the small group. After a moment, it flew straight at the doctor.

The doctor immediately grabbed C.J. by the collar and hauled him in close and used him as a shield from the wraith. He raised the knife until it was right under C.J.'s chin.

"Everyone stay back," he yelled, both to the wraith and the military men. "If anyone makes a move against me, the kid will be the first to die."

The wraith instantly stopped. Despite not understanding English, the wraith understood what the knife was and what it could do to its new friend.

"Please," Angus said, "let my son go. Won't stop you from leaving."

The doctor just laughed. "Once I am out of this pyramid and on my way down the mountain," he said, "I'll consider letting him go."

He caught a slight movement by one soldier. He turned his head slightly but kept C.J. between him and the wraith.

"I mean it," he said. "I will kill the boy. The meddling little brat messed up my whole operation. Don't think for a moment that I'd lose any sleep over killing him or any of you."

"You mean the gold," Angus said.

"Yes, the gold," Eberhardt said. "That wall is full of it. This whole mountain is full of it."

Eberhardt started backing up and dragged C.J. with him. The boy could feel the point of the knife dig into his throat. He didn't even want to swallow in fear that the knife might dig in further. Eberhardt maneuvered himself so that he was backing toward the door.

"This isn't just about escape," Angus said. "You could have tried other ways to escape. This is about revenge against my son."

"You're a bright one," Eberhardt said, laughing.

"You're going to kill him either way," Angus said.

Eberhardt smirked at Angus, but said nothing.

The wraith followed as he went through the door.

C.J. looked helplessly at his father.

Once he was out the door, Eberhardt yelled to everyone. "Stay where you are for one hour. If I see any of you come after me, I will make his death an extremely painful one."

Trying to use the boy to block the wraith from moving around him slowed his progress across the outer room.

Just as he placed his foot on the first step, the smile left his face. There was a sound on the steps just behind him.

C.J.'s heart leapt when he heard it. The low growling of a dog rumbled through the room. Even though he couldn't see it, C.J. knew that it was the black dog.

Eberhardt glanced quickly over his shoulder. The dog was standing on the steps above him, baring his teeth. He quickly pushed C.J. forward, away from the steps again and toward the wraith. The wraith drew away so as not to come in contact with C.J.

In Eberhardt's haste to regain his position, C.J. noticed that the knife had pulled away from his throat and the man's grip on him had loosened. He waited to see if the knife would drop just a little more.

It did.

C.J. dropped through the man's arms and wrenched away from the doctor's grip on his shoulder as he fell to the floor. He hit the floor and rolled away from the man. He rolled until he hit a wall and stopped.

Angus and the others rushed forward and crowded together at the doorway to see what was happening. Angus stepped toward C.J., but Roland held him back.

"Wait," Roland said, "not yet."

C.J., still lying on the floor next to the wall, looked up at the doctor.

The man found himself suddenly without protection, facing the black dog on one side and the wraith on the other. With no other options, he ran toward the steps and the black dog.

The dog stood its ground on the steps, growling. The doctor tried several times to push past the dog but only ended up retreating after it snapped at him each time.

Helplessly, he turned toward the wraith that had grown extremely large in the room. With a look of utter terror, the doctor pleaded with the wraith. He cried as he begged.

C.J. closed his eyes.

The wraith flew at the man and enveloped him. The man started screaming as he disappeared into the shadow of the wraith. He writhed in pain as the wraith continued to revolve around him, looking like a miniature tornado. The screams went on forever.

The lieutenant shouted orders for his men to take the kids back into the room, so they didn't see what was happening to Eberhardt. Laura and Scotty went with them, preferring not to see. Sadie shrugged out of their grasp so that she could watch until C.J. was safe. Frederick also stayed because what the wraith was doing fascinated him.

C.J. held his hands over his ears. "Stop!" C.J. yelled, barely audible above the man's screams. "Stop torturing him," he yelled louder.

The screams stopped, and it was suddenly unusually quiet. The wraith pulled away from the man. The shriveled up figure that stood there in the doctor's place looked as if he were well over 100 years old. A moment later, he fell to the floor, dead.

The dog went over to C.J. and nudged him. C.J. stood up and glanced at the body on the floor, but then quickly looked away. The dog guided him back into the sarcophagi room. Everyone fell back to make way for them, and his father grabbed his son and hugged him tightly.

The wraith also glided into the room. C.J. and his father backed up and stopped by the boy mummy in the center of the room. The wraith followed them and stopped next to the mummy, too. After a few moments, the image of the Inca boy replaced the darkness of the wraith once again.

The dog left C.J. and sat down beside the Inca boy and waited.

C.J. looked at the boy and the dog beside him and smiled. He pulled away from his father's embrace and faced the boy.

The boy looked down at the mummified body on the stone block and then picked something up off the folds of cloth. The pair of pyramidal dice that he had paused over earlier floated through the air on the boy's insubstantial palm and then hovered in front of C.J., waiting.

C.J. held out his hand, and the dice dropped from the boy's transparent hand into C.J.'s solid one. C.J. looked at the boy and nodded his thanks.

The boy then turned and, with the dog, walked to the doorway of the room. There, he paused, turned back, and waved. C.J. waved back.

The boy turned away again, and the dog led him across the room. As they crossed toward the steps, they both faded away and were gone.

Chapter 16

The guards at the entrance were ready when the group filed out of the pyramid. They relaxed when they saw the lieutenant and gave him their report.

One of them said something in Spanish, but the only word that C.J. caught was Eberhardt. The lieutenant filled them in about what happened in the pyramid and about Eberhardt's fate. All three fell silent as the other men filed by, carrying the bodies of the five men.

The lieutenant talked to Angus about the bodies. "Will you want to bury them in Peru?" he asked.

"No," Angus told him. "We'll take their bodies back to the States."

The lieutenant nodded and turned to leave. But Angus had another request before he went.

"There is one more man that Freitag told us about," Angus said. "They lost him somewhere in the pyramid. We would like to make an official report in case they find his body in the future."

"I will take care of that," he said and went off to join his men.

As the group crossed the plateau, the remaining members of Angus's team rushed over to greet them. Angus told them what had happened in the pyramid.

Laura's mother gave her a big hug first, followed by her father, Jackson. Teresa took her back, and the cycle continued for several minutes.

Walter and Edna enveloped their children in one big group hug. C.J. could hear them murmuring something to the two kids, but he was too far away to hear what they said. That group hug lasted a long time.

Even Axel put an arm around his son, Frederick, and told him he was proud of him. In all the time that C.J. had known them, this was the first time that he had seen Frederick's father show any emotion toward his son.

C.J. himself got another hug from his father.

"I thought that I'd lost you this time," Angus told him. "When Eberhardt grabbed you..." His voice trailed off.

"I know," C.J. said. "I thought that was it, too."

The lieutenant returned after the meeting with the men in his unit.

"We are heading back to Lima," the man told Angus. "I will make my official report to my commander in the morning."

"What will you report?" Angus asked.

The lieutenant glanced at the pyramid. "I don't think they will believe me, but I will report exactly what happened."

"Will we have to stay for a hearing?"

"I don't know," the lieutenant told him.

"We'll return to our ship tomorrow," Angus said. "In the morning, we need to clean up this site and remove our colleagues' equipment. After that, we'll wait on our ship for word from you."

"Very well," the lieutenant said. "Good bye, Dr. Kask," he said and shook Angus's hand.

He was about to turn away, but turned to C.J. instead. "I am happy to have met you," he said. C.J. shook his hand and smiled.

They watched as the lieutenant and his men mounted their horses with Freitag behind one of them, his hands tied. They waved as the unit made their way down the mountainside.

When they woke the next morning, the plateau had a wholly different feeling. With no one else but their group camping on the site and the wraith laid to rest, the sunny day seemed brighter, and they noticed sounds of bird calls and wind blowing through the trees below them.

The bonfire was out, and none of them were worried about the pyramid or anything inside. They set about making breakfast with the original expedition's supplies. No one rushed through the meal and the conversation stayed away from the events of the past days. They concentrated instead on the trip home.

After breakfast, they set about breaking down the camp and packing up all the supplies and equipment that were on site. They cleaned out the hidden room in the temple and, after discovering the antenna in the temple ruins, packed up the telegraph machine.

They returned all the rocks that the original expedition had collected to the sarcophagi room in the pyramid.

It took them several trips to haul everything down the mountainside to the truck, but by late afternoon, the plateau had been cleared of anything that would show they had been there.

As they made their last trip down, C.J. took one last look around the plateau. He imagined what the place would have looked like five hundred years earlier when the Inca were there, and the Inca boy was alive. Then he followed the others down the path.

When they reached the truck, they wasted no time and loaded everyone into it. Roland drove it back down and then north along the coast toward Lima.

Sadie saw C.J. gazing up at the peaks. "What are you thinking about?" she asked.

"Just looking at the mountains," C.J. said. "I wonder how many other burial places there are up there."

"Quite a few," Sadie said, looking up at the beautiful peaks of the Andes.

"How many other wraiths are waiting in them?"

They silently watched the mountains go by.

The truck pulled up to the docks near the Falcon, and everyone climbed out. They unloaded the truck onto the dock and then carried everything on board while Roland drove off to return the truck.

The young explorers silently watched the adults carry the remains of the original expedition aboard the ship and stow them below decks. Then, they pitched in to finish loading everything else on board.

When they were done, they gathered on the deck of the ship to wait until it was ready to leave. They watched the city as its people went about the evening. None of the residents of Lima were aware of the danger that had been so close to them for so long.

A military vehicle pulled up to the dock.

C.J. went to the door of the saloon. "Dad," he called. "There are some soldiers here."

Angus came out to meet them. It turned out to be the lieutenant and several other men. They greeted each other, and the lieutenant got down to business.

"Freitag has confessed and has given a full statement about what happened at the temple," he told them. "There will be no need for you to stay."

"That's good," Angus said. "What will happen?"

"They will charge him with attempted theft and smuggling of national artifacts," the lieutenant told him. "He will spend some time in prison and then the United States can extradite him for whatever charges they want to file. Once he leaves Peru, he can not come back."

"Thank you for your help," Angus told him as they shook hands.

"I hope your journey home is without incident," the lieutenant said. He and his men returned to their vehicle and drove off.

At sunset, the ship steamed out of the harbor. The kids watched the lights of the city come on as the coast of Peru disappeared into the distance.

After a while, there wasn't anything left to see in the dark. They were getting chilled by the night breeze, so they went back into the saloon. They found all the adults sitting about the room relaxing. It was a stark contrast to how they had spent their time on the trip down.

Angus called his son over to where he, Roland, and Walter were talking.

"You've been on several of our expeditions now, haven't you?" Angus asked.

C.J. nodded. His dad knew he had been.

"Each time, you and the other kids have come along as family of team members," Angus continued.

C.J. nodded again. He wasn't sure what his father was trying to say.

"Well, we've been talking and have decided that is going to change," Roland told him.

"You're not letting us come with you?" C.J. asked.

"We're going to let you come with us," Angus said, "but not as family members. We've decided that the five of you will officially be junior team members."

"You'll be our Young Explorers," Walter told him.

Angus gave him five patches just like the ones the adults had attached to their jackets to show that they were members of Kask's Expedition Team. Except theirs designated them as Junior Team Members.

C.J. looked at the patches and smiled.

"Go on," Angus said. "You can tell the others."

C.J. rushed off with the patches in hand.

He found Laura in a corner reading a book, with Scotty sitting nearby. He noticed Laura had a tan wool blanket covering her legs.

"You got your alpaca blanket?" C.J. asked.

"My mom got it for me," she said, smiling. "She thought it might take my mind off our worries."

"Worries about what?"

"About what?" she asked and threw a cushion at him. "We were all worried about the five of you sneaking around in the pyramid."

C.J. caught the cushion and laughed. He told them the news about being junior team members.

"You're the one who did everything," Scotty said. "We didn't help that much."

C.J. told him he was wrong. "If it weren't for what you knew about the architecture of the temple and pyramid and Laura's knowledge of languages, I wouldn't have been able to figure out what to do."

Scotty smiled and admired the patch. Laura put her book down and looked at her patch, too. They were both proud to be members of the team.

Frederick was talking with his father when C.J. interrupted them. He showed Frederick the patch and told him he was an official member of the team.

He looked at the patch but said nothing. The small smile that appeared on his face told C.J. that he was pleased.

"Thank you for your help yesterday," C.J. told him. "We wouldn't have escaped without you."

"Any time," Frederick said in a quiet voice as he gazed at the patch. Then, he realized what he had said and looked up at C.J. "It changes nothing," he said.

C.J. just smiled at him and then went to find Sadie.

Sadie was outside, watching the moonlight on the ocean. C.J. gave her the patch and told her the news.

"That's wonderful," Sadie said. "I'm proud of all of us." She looked up at C.J. "I'm especially proud of you. I'm glad you were right about the wraith."

"I'm glad that you..." C.J. started, "I mean, I'm glad no one got hurt."

Sadie gave him a quick kiss on the cheek and went over to the railing. After recovering from his surprise, C.J. joined her.

He put his patch in his pocket and found the rock that he had hidden from Eberhardt. He took it out and looked at it in the bright moonlight.

"A souvenir of our adventure?" Sadie asked.

"I guess so," C.J. said. He placed the rock back in his pocket and leaned on the railing.

He looked out onto the ocean and said, "I can't wait to see what our next adventure will be.

Don't miss out!

Visit the website below and you can sign up to receive emails whenever S T Cameron publishes a new book. There's no charge and no obligation.

https://books2read.com/r/B-A-CWRB-KEZQG

BOOKS 2 READ

Connecting independent readers to independent writers.

Also by S T Cameron

The Young Explorers
Inca Wraith
Phantom Express
Scottish Knight

Watch for more at www.stcameron.com.

About the Author

I tell stories and have adventures.When I was a little boy, I would tell stories and have adventures in the backyard pretending I was in a circus in front of an audience of my family and neighbors. In elementary school, more stories and adventures were played out on the stage in front of my class and, sometimes, the entire school.In High School and College, I donned my glasses and disguised my super writer self in my computer nerd persona and while I still told stories and had adventures, they were never made publicly known.Many years later, I decided that it was time to remove my disguise and let my stories out in the world again.Outside of writing, I have adventures with Kay, my wife and future author of her own books, my two wonderful daughters and their families including four grand-children and two grand-puppies. I also let people know what is going on with my writing at stcameron.com.

Read more at www.stcameron.com.